MYSTERY OF THE SAMURAI SWORD

Mystery of the Samurai Sword

Franklin W. Dixon

Illustrated by
Leslie Morrill

WANDERER BOOKS
New York

Manufactured in the United States of America
10 9 8 7 6 5 4

Wanderer and colophon are trademarks of Simon & Schuster

THE HARDY BOYS is a trademark of Stratemeyer Syndicate,
registered in the United States Patent and Trademark Office.

Library of Congress Cataloging in Publication Data

Dixon, Franklin W
Mystery of the Samurai Sword.

(Hardy boys mystery stories)
SUMMARY: A Japanese business tycoon mysteriously
disappears and, soon after, a rare samurai sword is stolen
from an art gallery. Suspecting a connection, the
Hardy boys try to solve the mystery.
[1. Mystery and detective stories]   I. Title.
PZ7.D644Myk 1979b   [Fic]   79-17392

ISBN 0-671-95506-3
ISBN 0-671-95497-0 pbk.

Contents

1 Mysterious Flashes   1
2 Telltale Splashes   9
3 The Face at the Window   17
4 A Trio of Suspects   25
5 A Breakneck Race   36
6 Flat-Out Finish   47
7 Cat Burglars   53
8 Invisible Men   63
9 Lurking Shadows   71
10 Trouble in Tokyo   80
11 A Crooked Offer   88
12 A Meeting at Midnight   94
13 Masked Riders   102
14 A Siren Shrieks!   114
15 Police Tip   123
16 A Startling Challenger   133
17 Jungle Nightmare   143
18 Gang Wheels   154
19 The Fearless Three   161
20 Black Commandos   169

1

Mysterious Flashes

Gusty sheets of rain swept the Bayport airfield. The moon had disappeared behind a heavy overcast sky, but the glare of floodlights lit the airport with almost daytime brilliance.

A little knot of people, huddling beneath umbrellas, watched eagerly as a small jet plane swooped out of the darkness and braked to a screaming halt between the twin rows of landing lights.

"Just a few seconds till ten o'clock," announced dark-haired, eighteen-year-old Frank Hardy with a glance at his wristwatch. "Mr. Satoya's right on the button!"

"Hey, what's going on over there?" muttered his blond brother, Joe, who was a year younger.

Through the rain-washed glass front of the airport

1

terminal wing, a bearded man could be seen gesticulating wildly. He was waving a long, sheathed sword over his head.

"Looks like a Japanese samurai sword," said Frank.

"Sure does! But what's wrong with the guy?" Joe wondered aloud. "Is he doing a war dance or just trying to attract our attention?"

Before Frank could reply, a policeman appeared and hustled the man away despite his protests.

Meanwhile, an unloading ramp had been wheeled up to the executive jet, which bore the famous red-and-white emblem of the Satoya Corporation—a samurai sword curving beneath the rising sun.

"Have you ever seen Mr. Satoya before, Dad?" Frank asked his father, who stood next to the boys.

Fenton Hardy shook his head. "No. Very few people have in recent years. He runs a worldwide business, but has become almost a hermit. In fact he has seldom been photographed."

"Sounds like quite a mystery man!"

"You could call him that, I suppose. Actually that's what a good many reporters and magazine writers *do* call him—just because he's so hard to see or interview."

"Who do you suppose leaked news of his trip to the press?" put in Joe.

"Good question," his father replied grimly. "I intend to find out the answer. His company wanted this visit to America kept top secret, and we've done everything possible to maintain tight security at this end."

The tall, distinguished-looking detective, formerly an ace investigator with the New York Police Department, had been hired to protect the Japanese tycoon from assassins or terrorists during his stay in the United States. But despite Mr. Hardy's efforts to ensure secrecy, a number of reporters had shown up at the airport to witness Satoya's arrival. Luckily the police were keeping them at a distance.

Two men were allowed through the barrier and joined Mr. Hardy and his sons. One was the detective's longtime operative, Sam Radley, the other a burly six-foot Japanese named Kawanishi. He was a Satoya executive, who had flown to the United States with a colleague a few days earlier to arrange details of the trip.

Just then an erect, gray-haired man with a wispy mustache emerged from the plane.

"Ah! That is my revered employer, Mr. Takashi Satoya," Kawanishi said. After greeting the tycoon in Japanese, he introduced him to the Hardys and Sam Radley.

A younger man had followed Satoya down the ramp. He turned out to be another executive of the firm, but of lower rank than Kawanishi. His name was Ikeda. He was slim and strongly built, and his black hair was cut very short.

"I suggest we get underway as soon as your car is unloaded, sir," Mr. Hardy said to Satoya.

The tycoon nodded courteously. "Whatever you say,

Mr. Hardy. Our security is in your hands from this point on."

A cargo hatch had already been opened in the executive jet, and a sleek black limousine was driven out of the plane's interior and down a ramp onto the airfield. It was bigger and longer than most Japanese cars. Joe whistled admiringly as a granite-faced chauffeur drove it smoothly toward the group. "Some job!"

"You can say that again," Frank agreed. "Must have been specially built."

Mr. Satoya and his junior aide, Ikeda, took their places in the back seat of the limousine. Sam Radley was allowed, rather grudgingly it seemed, to sit in front beside the chauffeur.

The burly senior aide, Kawanishi, was to ride in Mr. Hardy's car behind the limousine, while a state policeman of the highway patrol would clear the way on a motorcycle at the head of the procession.

Frank and Joe, also mounted on motorcycles, had been assigned to act as outriders.

"Keep a sharp eye open for trouble anywhere along the route into town," the detective told his sons before taking the wheel of his car.

"Will do, Dad!" Joe replied.

"I'm glad we wore our raingear," Frank murmured as the two boys started toward their road bikes.

"We'll probably get soaked anyhow," said Joe. "One good thing, though—this rain should cut down the traffic quite a bit."

At a radio signal from Fenton Hardy, the little motorcade got underway, tooling along the exit road that led out of the airport. Once on the open highway, the vehicles picked up speed. The motorcade rolled along smoothly for several miles. But as the expressway wound through a hilly stretch, the state policeman waved his hand in a sudden warning signal.

Frank and Joe heard his voice come over their CB radios: "Looks like a little tie-up!"

Two or three cars had slowed to a halt just ahead. The policeman steered his motorcycle past them to find the reason for the delay. Frank and Joe followed suit. They braked as they saw a tree lying across the road.

"The storm must have blown it down off the hillside," Frank opined.

"What's the trouble, fellows?" Fenton Hardy's voice crackled on the radio.

"Tree down. Nothing serious, Dad," Joe replied. "We'll be moving again soon."

Dismounting, the Hardys lent the policeman a hand in clearing the obstruction. The windfallen tree was little more than a sapling, but somewhat awkward for one man to handle.

As soon as it was out of the way, the cars began to roll again. Frank and Joe were about to climb back on their motorcycles when a brilliant light flashed from the hillside on the right.

"What was that?" Joe exclaimed.

Two more dazzling flashes exploded in quick succession.

"Must be a photographer!" Frank guessed.

"You're right!" Joe blurted. "Snapping pictures of Mr. Satoya, I'll bet!"

As their vision recovered from the flashes, they saw a figure burst from cover and sprint up the muddy hillside in the darkness. The Hardys wanted to leave their bikes and take off in angry pursuit but horns began to honk impatiently as more and more cars lined up behind them.

"No law against taking pictures," said the state policeman philosophically.

"Guess you're right," Frank agreed with a disgusted look. "Too bad we can't prove he planted that roadblock."

The Hardys and the policeman gunned their cycles into action again, and the motorcade resumed its swift journey into Bayport.

They passed through the outskirts and soon reached the downtown area. The rain had subsided, and the wet pavement glistened under the street lights.

As they neared the Bayport Chilton Hotel, Joe saw a short, thickset, broad-shouldered Japanese come out and stand beside the doorman to watch the approaching motorcade. He was Mr. Oyama, who had flown to the USA with Mr. Kawanishi to prepare for their employer's visit.

Oyama was wearing a radio headset and had a small

7

transceiver tucked in his breast pocket. Joe guessed that Satoya's chauffeur must have transmitted word of their arrival.

The sleek black limousine drew up directly in front of the hotel entrance canopy. Mr. Hardy's car stopped behind it, while his two sons and the highway patrolman found parking places for their motorcycles along the curb.

The chauffeur was the first to leap out. Sam Radley, Fenton Hardy and Mr. Kawanishi followed suit, while a little knot of onlookers gathered to goggle at the VIP in the limousine. Waving the doorman away, the chauffeur moved swiftly to open the back door of the car. He stood stiffly at attention, waiting for his master to get out. But Satoya did not emerge from the limousine!

Fenton Hardy and Mr. Kawanishi reacted simultaneously, guessing that something was wrong. They almost bumped heads as they bent forward to peer into the car's rear passenger compartment.

"What's the matter, Dad?" Frank exclaimed, noticing his father's startled expression.

A moment later, as the Hardy boys pressed closer, they could see for themselves the reason for the men's dismay.

The young executive named Ikeda lay slumped unconscious in the back seat of the limousine, and Mr. Satoya had disappeared!

2

Telltale Splashes

The news spread like wildfire among the bystanders. They pressed closer, exclaiming excitedly.

"What about Mr. Ikeda, Dad?" Joe asked.

"Looks like he's been drugged," said Mr. Hardy after thumbing back the victim's eyelids to examine his pupils. "Go get the hotel doctor, Joe—this man may need attention."

The medic quickly arrived on the scene. He confirmed Mr. Hardy's opinion, but stated that Ikeda would probably sleep off the anesthetic without any ill effects.

Seeing the unconscious Japanese being carried into the hotel stirred fresh excitement among the sidewalk crowd. Luckily the highway patrolman was able to hold them back.

"You've no idea what happened, Sam?" Fenton Hardy asked his operative.

"Not a clue," Radley confessed, looking chagrined and mystified. "The dark partition between the front and back seats is a one-way glass pane. When you're sitting in front, you can't see into the rear passenger compartment at all."

The driver, he explained, relied on a wide-angle roof periscope for his view of the road behind instead of a rearview mirror.

"Could Mr. Satoya have jumped out when we stopped on the highway to remove that tree?" Frank inquired.

Mr. Hardy frowned. "Seems to be the only possible answer, but my car was right behind the limousine. I can't believe he got out without either Mr. Kawanishi or myself spotting him."

The burly Japanese agreed and added, "Unfortunately the chauffeur, Shigemi, doesn't speak much English. But I questioned him while the doctor was examining Ikeda, and he can shed no light on the mystery."

Frank glanced at the stony-faced driver and wondered if he knew more than he was telling. But his impassive expression gave no hint of whatever thoughts might be passing through his head.

"Think you would have noticed if the back door had been opened on either side?" Joe asked Sam Radley.

The private eye hesitated before nodding unhappily. "Yes, I do. But it's hard to be sure."

Mr. Oyama, the other senior aide, exchanged a few words in Japanese with the chauffeur and then turned back to the Americans.

"A red light on the dashboard flashes if either back door is opened, or even if one becomes unlatched," he pointed out. "Shigemi is quite certain no such thing happened."

"That's assuming the flasher works," Mr. Hardy countered shrewdly. "Better have him check it to make sure."

Oyama transmitted the order in Japanese. The chauffeur touched his cap in a silent salute, then closed the car doors and climbed back behind the wheel. He drove the limousine past the hotel, then turned down a ramp which led to an underground parking garage.

By now reporters and television news crews, who had been unable to interview Mr. Satoya at the airport, were arriving at the hotel. They crowded around the detectives and the two Japanese aides, bombarding them with questions and adding to the noisy confusion.

"What do you make of it, Frank?" Joe asked.

"I have no idea," Frank said, "but this sure puts Dad on the spot!"

"I'll say it does," Joe agreed as they made their way into the hotel lobby. "The Satoya Corporation hires him to protect the head of their company—and now Satoya disappears less than an hour after he lands!

Boy, that'll really look bad in the news stories wh—"

Frank flashed his brother a quizzical glance as the younger Hardy boy suddenly broke off. "What's the matter, Joe?"

"Over there by the reception desk," Joe pointed. "It's that nut we saw at the airport, waving a sword!"

"Hey, you're right! Now's our chance to find out what he wanted!"

The bearded man had just peeled off his tan raincoat. He was folding it and laying it on top of his suitcases while he waited to check in behind two other newly arrived guests. As he straightened up, he saw the Hardys striding toward him, and his face took on an embarrassed, furtive expression.

"We're Frank and Joe Hardy, two of Mr. Satoya's escorts," the older boy said. "Would you mind telling us why you were waving that sword at the airport?"

The man's face reddened and his prominent nose seemed to twitch nervously like a rabbit's. He had a wild mop of curly hair, the same sandy color as his whiskers, which somehow added to his look of comic confusion.

"Well, uh, actually it was just a spur of the moment advertising tactic, you might say." The man chuckled, then gulped. "I was hoping I might make a lucky sale."

"A lucky *sale?*" Joe regarded him with a puzzled frown. "A sale of what?"

"The samurai sword you saw. It's a *katana,* or long sword, of excellent workmanship, dating from the

12

early eighteenth century. I thought if I could catch Satoya's eye, he might be interested enough to buy it."

The man bent down and opened the larger of his two suitcases so the boys could look inside. To their astonishment, they saw that it contained a number of sheathed swords and daggers. "That's my business—selling Oriental art objects—but as you see, I specialize in fine blades."

Snapping his suitcase shut again, the man plucked a card from his wallet and handed it to the Hardys. It bore the name *Axel Gorky* with a phone number and cable address in Boston.

Joe said, "How did you know Mr. Satoya was coming to Bayport?"

"But I didn't," Gorky replied, looking surprised at the question. "Had I known, I would have written beforehand to ask for a proper appointment! I myself just arrived in Bayport this evening, a short time before he did. When I saw the TV camera crews, I asked what was going on. Someone told me this famous Japanese industrialist was about to land—so I seized my chance."

Gorky's face went pink again. "Perhaps I did make a fool of myself, waving the sword as I did—but then one has to catch the customer's attention in order to make a sale."

"Any objection to telling us your business here in Bayport?" Frank asked stolidly.

"Of course not. I came to call on several customers—including the dancer Warlord. As you probably know, he uses various knives and swords in some of his dance numbers."

Just then the two guests in front of him finished registering at the hotel desk. Gorky excused himself and moved up to sign for a room. He looked relieved at the chance to get away from the Hardys.

"Think he was leveling with us?" Joe muttered as the boys started back across the lobby.

Frank grinned dryly. "His story's so nutty I'm inclined to buy it. Anyhow, he's checking in at the Chilton, so we'll know where to find him if we want to ask him more questions."

Just then they saw their father and Mr. Kawanishi come into the hotel, accompanied by Chief Collig, head of the Bayport police force. Newsmen swarmed in after them, trying to snap pictures and pick up additional morsels of information for the next morning's headline stories on the Japanese tycoon's sensational disappearance.

"No use trying to talk to Dad," Frank said. "Let's see what's doing outside."

"Okay."

A bigger crowd than before was milling about the sidewalk, a couple of plainclothes detectives circulating among them. The Hardy boys saw Sam Radley conferring with the state policeman and trying to fend off other news hawks.

The boys shucked their raincoats, rolled them up and stuffed them into their motorcycle pouches.

"Oh, oh!" Frank suddenly murmured under his breath.

Joe glanced up at his brother. "What's the matter?"

"Take a look at that photographer."

"Where?"

"Over there. The one snapping a picture of the motorcycle cop."

"What about him?"

Frank drew his brother closer to the man in question. The photographer was using an expensive Japanese-made 35-millimeter camera and a "potato-masher" flash unit powerful enough for long-range shots at night.

Joe looked at Frank, puzzled. "I don't get it. What am I supposed to see?"

"Those mud stains on his pants," Frank whispered.

The man's trouser legs were splashed up to the knees. Even his raincoat bore a few muddy traces.

"Wow!" Joe hissed. "He could've been that guy on the hillside who snapped pictures when we were coming in from the airport!"

Joe's muted exclamation carried farther than he expected. The photographer whirled around and stared at the boys suspiciously. The next instant he dashed off across the street!

"After him!" Frank cried.

The Hardys took off in hot pursuit. Their quarry was already disappearing down the block. He was a healthy-looking young man in his early twenties, and now he was whizzing away from them with long-legged trip-hammer strides. Frank and Joe could hardly keep him in sight!

He rounded the next corner into a dark side street. The Hardys made a skidding turn and continued the chase, though for the moment neither could see the fugitive ahead.

Their pursuit might have ended in failure had Joe not glimpsed a movement out of the corner of his eye. Glancing toward the building on his left, he saw a figure huddled in a darkened doorway.

"Hold it, Frank!" Joe shouted, braking hard with shoe leather. "I think I've found him!"

A moment later, as Joe lunged toward the doorway, he caught a fist square in the face!

3

The Face at the Window

The blow was too hasty to have much force, but it landed hard enough to knock Joe off balance. He grabbed the photographer's raincoat to steady himself, and by hanging on like a bulldog, kept the man from getting away.

By this time Frank had reached the scene. For a few moments fists flew in all directions. But their quarry soon realized he was cornered and gave up.

"Okay, okay, cool it, you two!" the photographer panted.

"You're the one who started swinging!" Frank retorted angrily.

"What did you expect me to do when two guys start chasing me down a dark street? Just stand still and get mugged?"

17

"Nobody's mugging you. We just wanted to ask you some questions."

"How did I know that?"

"If you had nothing to hide," put in Joe, "why did you run away from us?"

"Why should I have anything to hide? I've never even seen you before!"

"Oh no? How about on the highway tonight, when we were escorting Mr. Satoya's limousine in from the airport?"

The young photographer glared sullenly. "I don't know what you're talking about!"

"Can the innocent act!" Frank growled. "The film in your camera will prove whether or not you're the guy who snapped those flash photos on the hillside."

"So what if I did? There's no law against taking pictures."

"There is against blocking traffic—especially when you deliberately plant an obstruction on the open highway, like that tree you dragged across the road!"

"You can't prove that!"

"Look! We're not going to waste any more breath," Frank declared. "If you'd rather have us call the police, we will—and you can explain to them how it all happened. On the other hand, if you'd rather talk to us, we're willing to listen—and if you're not mixed up in anything crooked, we'll promise not to turn you in."

The photographer hesitated uncertainly, his glance

wavering back and forth between the two Hardy boys. Finally he made up his mind. "Okay, I'll talk . . . Not that I have much to tell you."

"We'll decide that," said Joe. "You know who we are?"

"Sure, you're the Hardy boys. From what I gather, your dad was hired to protect Satoya."

Frank's eyes narrowed. "Who told you that?"

The photographer shrugged. "Nobody in particular. It was just common gossip among the newsmen around here. Actually I heard a couple of reporters talking about it at the airport restaurant earlier this evening."

"Any idea where *they* picked it up?"

"I got the impression someone phoned a tip to one of the papers. He revealed the whole story about Satoya's visit to this country—including the fact that Fenton Hardy was supposed to keep him under wraps."

"You work for the *Bayport Herald?*" Joe asked.

"Nope, just a stringer for the wire services. I'm a freelancer."

The photographer, whose name turned out to be Pete Ogden, said he had devised and carried out his roadblock trick with the aid of a couple of members of the local Gung-Ho motorcycle gang. One had waited at the airport and called Ogden at a roadside phone booth to alert him as soon as the motorcade got underway for Bayport.

The other gang member had helped him maneuver

19

the fallen tree into position so that it could be toppled across the highway at short notice. Then the same youth had cycled back toward the airport and tipped off Ogden by walkie-talkie when he sighted Satoya's limousine and escorts.

"I figured if I could obtain a couple of good candid camera shots of Satoya," the photographer concluded, "they'd not only bring a high price, they might even help me land a job on one of the major newspapers."

"Wait a minute," Frank said with a thoughtful frown. "Did you *get* any good shots?"

"Dunno, I haven't developed them yet. But I sure hope so. I wanted to shoot some more pictures at the hotel, but it turned out that Satoya had disappeared."

"But do you think you *got* him?" Frank persisted.

Ogden scratched his head. "Well, I got somebody. There was a face in the window when the second and third flashes went off."

"But you're not sure whose? I mean, you couldn't describe the face?"

Ogden shook his head. "No way. It all happened too fast, and I was too excited."

Frank exchanged a look with Joe, who by now had caught the reason for his brother's questions.

"Leaping lizards!" the younger Hardy boy exclaimed. "If we could see those pictures, they might tell us whether or not Satoya jumped out during the traffic tie-up!"

Pete Ogden was not enthusiastic about sharing his

possibly valuable photos with the Hardys. But he realized that if he refused, the police were likely to seize his camera and impound the film as evidence. So he agreed to develop the roll immediately and allow Frank and Joe to inspect the results.

The Hardys and Ogden returned to the photographer's car, which was parked near the hotel. Then the two boys trailed him home on their motorcycles. He lived in a small flat above a bookstore on the edge of the downtown area.

Frank and Joe waited while he developed the film. The negatives were too small for them to recognize the face in the car window, even when viewed under a magnifying glass. So Ogden made an eight-by-ten enlargement of the best shot.

It showed that the person looking out of the limousine was definitely Satoya! He was wide-eyed and his mouth was partly open, portraying the typical expression of a subject surprised by a sudden photoflash.

"So he was in the car all right, even after we removed the tree!" Joe declared.

"And he sure doesn't look like he was about to hop out in the next few moments before we got underway again," Frank added.

Pete Ogden shot an excited glance at the Hardys. "Then you mean this photograph *proves* something about the mystery?"

Frank nodded. "I'd say it proves that Satoya did not disappear on the highway."

"Hey, how about that?" Ogden snapped his fingers triumphantly. "Maybe I can sell these shots for even more than I figured! Thanks a lot, you guys."

Outside Ogden's flat, the boys were about to climb back on their motorcycles when Joe suddenly stopped his brother. "Did you see something move just then?"

"Like what?"

"I don't know. A dark figure over there in the park."

"Matter of fact I did, but I thought I was imagining things. Let's take a look!"

The park was a triangular grassy island at the junction of three streets. The boys darted across to the island and spent several minutes searching among the few scattered trees and shrubbery, but could find no trace of anyone lurking there.

"That's funny," Joe said in frustration. "I could have sworn I saw someone dressed in black from head to toe!"

"Guess our imaginations were working overtime," Frank said. "You'll have to admit not many people except frogmen go around looking like that."

"Where to now?" said Joe, as they mounted their street bikes. "Report to Dad?"

"May as well." Frank hesitated. "You've read the Sherlock Holmes stories, haven't you, Joe?"

"Sure, even Dad likes them. He says Sherlock Holmes and Edgar Allan Poe's detective are the greatest masters of deduction that writers have ever dreamed up. Why'd you ask?"

"If you remember, one of Sherlock Holmes's rules was that when you've eliminated all the explanations of a mystery but one, then that one must be the answer—no matter how far out it seems."

Joe frowned. "So? What're you getting at?"

"Just this," Frank replied. "We didn't hit a single red light coming into Bayport tonight. And the only time we stopped was during the traffic tie-up. If Satoya didn't get out of the car then—"

"He must still have been inside when we got to the hotel!" Joe concluded excitedly. "That's straight thinking, Frank. And if no one could see him when the chauffeur opened the door—"

It was Frank's turn to finish the sentence. "Then he must have been *hiding* inside the car!"

"Which means there would have to be a secret compartment in the limousine. Let's go check it out right now!"

They reached the Bayport Chilton in three minutes. The crowd of curious onlookers had thinned considerably, and neither Fenton Hardy nor Sam Radley was anywhere in sight. The Hardys took an elevator to the parking garage in the basement.

The black limousine was easy to spot, but Joe stopped abruptly as they neared it.

"Hey, we'll probably need a key to get inside."

Without a word, Frank held one up.

"Dad slipped this to me before we left the airport. He arranged beforehand with Mr. Kawanishi to get three extra keys—one for himself, one for Sam, and one for you and me—so any of us could take over in a hurry and drive the limousine out of danger in case of emergency."

"Great!" said Joe. "Let's see what we can find."

Frank unlocked the limousine, and the Hardys proceeded to examine both the front and rear seat areas thoroughly. They marveled at the fine craftsmanship and fittings, but could discover no hiding place.

Finally Joe stepped back and scratched his head. "Hold it, Frank! Did you notice the distance between the back of the front seat and the dividing partition? You sure wouldn't need all that room just for upholstery or springs!"

"Right," Frank agreed. "And what's this little metal button for, right where the glass fits into the lower half of the partition? It can't be a rivet head bec—"

The next moment, as Frank's forefinger touched the metal button, both boys gasped.

The leather-covered lower half of the partition was slowly sliding upward over the glass pane!

4

A Trio of Suspects

The leather panel continued moving upward until the glass pane between the top of the front seat and the roof was completely covered.

The Hardy boys could now see a large hollow space between the back of the front seat and the rear passenger compartment, which the sliding panel had previously concealed!

"Leaping lizards! That's big enough for a man to hide in!" Joe exclaimed.

"Or big enough to stash a body in," Frank said grimly.

"You mean someone may have drugged Satoya, the same way Ikeda was drugged?" Joe frowned doubtfully. "But they were the only two people in the back seat."

"So far as we know," Frank countered. "But suppose someone else was hiding in this secret compartment when the limousine was driven off the plane?"

"You've got a point there," Joe conceded. "So the hidden perpetrator crawls out sometime before we get to Bayport, zaps both Ikeda and Satoya with a hypodermic needle or a whiff of gas and then stuffs Satoya's body into the secret compartment."

"Well, it's one possible scenario," said Frank in a dubious voice.

"Just one catch to it."

"Don't bother telling me, I already know."

"Namely, what happened to the dirty trickster who did all this?"

Frank grinned wryly. "Look, I came up with part of an answer—you're supposed to supply the rest."

"Okay," said Joe, rising to the challenge. "So maybe the guilty party was a midget or a dwarf. He not only stuffs Satoya's unconscious body into the secret compartment—he squirms back inside himself and then closes the sliding panel."

"Pretty tight fit, I'd say—unless he was about the size of Tom Thumb."

"Why not? Dwarfs can come pretty small."

"And after the limousine's parked in the garage, he hops out of the secret compartment again and carries off Satoya on his back."

Joe returned his brother's grin. "If you have a better answer, let's hear it."

"I think we're both getting wacko. Before we come up with any more goofy theories, there's one important point we should clear up, Joe."

"What's that?"

"Do Kawanishi and Oyama know about this secret compartment?"

"Hm, good question. Let's ask them."

The Hardys locked the limousine and returned to the elevator. From their earlier briefings by their father, they knew the location of the suite reserved for the visiting Japanese. They got out at the fifteenth floor and spoke to the security guard who had been stationed there at Mr. Hardy's orders.

"Is Dad around?" Frank inquired.

"Nope. Just Mr. Kawanishi and Mr. Oyama."

"We'd like to speak to them."

"Just a second." The guard announced them over a special phone that had been installed for this purpose, then nodded and gestured for the boys to proceed.

Mr. Kawanishi, the burly senior aide who had met the Hardys at the airport, opened the door to admit the two youths. His colleague, Mr. Oyama, was standing by a window overlooking the street. He turned to greet the boys when they entered.

"We have a question to ask you gentlemen, if you don't mind," Frank began.

"By all means," said Kawanishi. "If you lads or your father can do anything to clear up this appalling mystery, we shall be most grateful!"

27

"Did you know there's a secret compartment in Mr. Satoya's limousine?"

There was a silence, during which the two aides glanced at each other uncomfortably.

"Yes, we know about that," said Mr. Oyama. The squat, broad-shouldered Japanese gestured toward a sofa. "If you will please be seated, we shall try to explain."

The boys obeyed and waited to hear what their hosts had to say.

"Our revered employer designed that compartment himself," Mr. Kawanishi told them.

"What for?" asked Joe.

"As a way of eluding newsmen and inquisitive crowds."

"Wouldn't it be simpler to curtain the windows," said Frank, "or just have them made out of one-way glass, like the partition pane between the front and rear seat compartments?"

"So it might seem at first thought," Mr. Oyama replied. "But actually that would only whet people's curiosity. You have no idea how much interest and gossip Mr. Satoya has aroused by his secretive ways."

"In Tokyo," Mr. Kawanishi put in, "reporters will sometimes hover for hours around our central office building merely in the hope of glimpsing our employer or snapping his photo."

"If the interior of his limousine were hidden from view," Oyama went on, "they would assume he was

28

inside it, behind the curtains or the one-way glass. So they would try harder than ever to corner him."

"But if they see his car leave or arrive empty—or rather, *apparently* empty," the other aide added, "then his whereabouts remains a mystery. His pursuers are baffled and tend to become discouraged."

"I see." Frank frowned and digested this information thoughtfully.

Joe spoke up. "Why didn't you tell our father all this when the limousine first arrived at the hotel, and he discovered Mr. Satoya's disappearance?"

There was another awkward silence and exchange of glances between the two Japanese.

"You are right to take us to task," said Mr. Kawanishi, bowing his head contritely. "However, it occurred to both of us that Satoya-san might have become—how do you say?—camera shy, because of what happened on the way in from the airport. Therefore he might have chosen to conceal himself in the secret compartment for his own reasons."

"Naturally, in such a case," Mr. Oyama explained, "it would not have been right for us to go against our revered employer's wishes and reveal his hiding place."

This time it was the Hardy boys' turn to exchange glances. The reasoning of the two Orientals sounded logical enough, but it certainly clashed with their own impatient, practical Western outlook.

"What about Mr. Ikeda?" Frank questioned. "How did you think he got drugged or anesthetized? Or weren't you concerned about what happened to *him?*"

"He is very much junior to Satoya-san," Mr. Kawanishi pointed out patiently, as if he were correcting a child or a barbarian whose ignorance could be excused. "We were certainly disturbed to find him in such a condition. But that in itself would not excuse us from respecting our employer's wishes."

"In any case," Mr. Oyama said, "we had no intention of standing by and doing nothing. Perhaps you may recall that I left the scene soon after the chauffeur drove off."

"What did you do?" Joe asked.

"I hurried down to the garage by elevator in order to be on hand when the limousine pulled in. I wished to see for myself whether Satoya-san had concealed himself in the secret compartment."

Frank said, "And what did you find?"

Oyama spread his hands in a helpless shrug. "Nothing. The compartment was empty."

The Hardys thanked the two senior aides for their time and went down to the lobby, where they failed to find their father. As they left the hotel, they encountered a couple of their high school buddies, Tony Prito and pudgy Chet Morton.

Joe hailed them. "Hey, what're you guys doing downtown so late?"

"Checking out the new disco," Tony replied. "Then we heard a midnight news broadcast on the car radio about that Japanese big shot disappearing, so we hustled over to get the scoop. He was a client of your dad's, wasn't he?"

"*Is* a client," Frank corrected. "Tony, don't jinx him by putting him in the past tense!"

"Never mind all that! What happened to the guy?" Chet blurted. "Did some dragon society snatch him for violating its sacred customs?"

Joe grinned. "You're a little mixed up, Chester. The way we heard it, dragon societies and tongs are Chinese. Satoya comes from Japan. There's a slight difference."

"So what? They're both Oriental, aren't they? Quit stalling and give us the lowdown on this case!"

"I wish we could, Chet," Frank confessed wryly. "But if you want the latest bulletin, Mr. Satoya's still missing, and his disappearance remains as much of a mystery as ever. You can quote us."

"You mean you Hardys are baffled?"

"Put it this way," said Joe. "We're working on it."

"How about stopping off at the diner for a couple of burgers and a milkshake?" Chet proposed. "Then you can fill us in on the details."

"Got a better idea," Joe countered. "Aunt Gertrude's probably still up, waiting for a blow-by-blow account of the mystery. How about stopping off at our place, and maybe we can talk her out of some apple pie in return for a firsthand report."

"It's a deal!"

Gertrude Hardy, who lived with Frank and Joe and

31

their parents, was Fenton Hardy's unmarried sister. The tall, bony spinster worried constantly about the safety of the famed detective and her two nephews. Yet, despite her constant prophecies of looming danger, she kept herself avidly up to date on all their latest sleuthing activities.

More important from Chet's point of view, she was also one of the best cooks and bakers in Bayport. The Hardy boys found her fretfully awaiting their return, wrapped in her red bathrobe, with her hair in curlers.

"Chet and Tony are with us, Aunt Gertrude," Joe said. "Mind if they come in?"

"Of course not!" she said sharply. "They're probably as hungry as you two. I'd much rather you all did your late snacking here than out in some rowdy drive-in!"

"Well, if you insist, Miss Hardy!" said plump Chet Morton, eagerly pressing forward into the kitchen behind Frank and Joe.

Soon all four boys were hungrily attacking thick Dagwood sandwiches and slices of fresh apple pie, washing them down with glasses of milk.

"Where's Mom?" Frank asked between bites.

"In bed, where all you young ones should be at this hour!" Aunt Gertrude retorted. "She has to get up early tomorrow to help prepare the Garden Club display at the Bayport Festival. For that matter, where's your father?"

"Dunno, Aunty," Frank replied. "Last we saw of him, he was pretty busy coping with what happened tonight."

"Well, for mercy sakes, what did happen? I couldn't make head or tail out of the news broadcasts!"

The Hardy boys described the strange disappearance of Takashi Satoya, and their own subsequent adventures. The bathrobed spinster listened with keen interest.

"Hmph, sounds to me as though Satoya's been snatched by business enemies!" she declared. "Not surprising either, when you stop to think how big a corporation he's running. That's probably why he's been hiding from public view. He knew someone was out to get him."

"I'll buy that about someone being out to get him," Chet piped up. "If you ask me, it's probably a mysterious gang of Oriental killers!"

"Such as?" Joe said.

"How do I know? Maybe that creep you spotted who was all in black could be one of them!"

"*If* we spotted him," Frank amended. "But none of that explains how Satoya vanished."

"Those flashes in the darkness could have blinded everyone for a second or two while you were stopped on the highway," Aunt Gertrude pointed out. "Perhaps that was long enough for a kidnapper to drag him out of the car before you got going again."

"What about his aide Ikeda, who was drugged?"

"Perhaps the kidnapper had a confederate who jabbed him with a hypodermic needle."

"Hm, it's an interesting theory," Frank said politely if a bit skeptically.

Just then a car was heard pulling into the driveway. Soon afterward Fenton Hardy strode into the house. He greeted everyone in his usual friendly fashion, but Frank and Joe could see that their father was both angry and deeply concerned over the night's events. However, his sons' report about the limousine's secret compartment made him feel somewhat better.

"What was Mr. Satoya planning to do in this country, Dad?" Frank inquired.

"Among other things, confer with officials of the Road King Motorcycle Company. There's talk of a merger between Road King and Satoya's own motorcycle division."

"You see? What did I tell you!" Aunt Gertrude cut in triumphantly. "A move like that could easily have stirred up business enemies!"

"Quite true," Mr. Hardy agreed. "What I'd like to lay hands on fast is the enemy in Satoya's own corporation."

"How do you mean, Dad?" Joe queried.

The detective rose from his chair to pace the kitchen floor. "Someone tipped off the press that Satoya was coming to this country. The tip came in the form of anonymous calls to the news services and networks, and naturally, since Satoya's such a mystery man, they were all eager to get a look at him. Yet I'm absolutely sure there was no leak in my security setup!"

"Then where did the leak occur?"

"It has to be in the Satoya Corporation," Mr. Hardy

replied. "Aside from the jet plane crew and his chauffeur, the only other people who knew in advance about his visit were Kawanishi, Oyama and Ikeda—though I'll admit it's hard to believe Ikeda would deliberately have landed himself in such an unpleasant predicament."

"So right off the bat," Frank reflected grimly, "we have at least three important suspects!"

Next day, the Hardy boys decided to check up on Axel Gorky's story. The best way to do this seemed to be to interview Warlord. The famous dancer and his troupe were to perform at the Bayport Summer Festival and were staying at Bayshore College, which was sponsoring their appearance.

The boys arrived on campus about 10:30 in the morning and were directed to the gymnasium, where the troupe was working out. As they entered the building vestibule, a loud, angry voice reached them from the gym floor.

"Maybe we came at the wrong time," Joe said. "Think we should go on in?"

"May as well," Frank said wryly. "I don't see any receptionist to announce us."

The boys had just started to walk through the doorway leading to the gym when a man came charging out, almost knocking them down in the process!

5

A Breakneck Race

Joe was the first to recover. "Watch it, mister!" he exclaimed. "Where's the fire?"

The man, who was strongly built, with freckled skin and thinning red hair, merely snorted and brushed past the two boys without the slightest apology.

"How do you like that?" Frank muttered in a taut voice. "The big ape doesn't even have manners enough to say 'Excuse me'!"

"I should've belted him one!" Joe fumed. "In fact maybe we ought to go after him and *demand* an apology."

"Forget it," Frank said, choking back his own temper. "That's not why we came."

The Hardys went on into the gymnasium, where half

a dozen dancers were going through various exercises—mostly practicing ballet movements or doing warm-up calisthenics. Two others were engaged in acrobatic flips and leaps under the critical gaze of a man with a lionlike mane of long black hair.

The boys recognized him from the festival posters as Warlord, whose real name was Yvor Killian. They caught his eye and he came over to see what they wanted.

Frank introduced himself and his brother and got an immediate smile of greeting.

"Of course! You're those famous young sleuths, the Hardy boys!" Warlord offered them each a handshake. "It's a pleasure to meet such noted manhunters! Don't tell me you're here on the trail of a new mystery?"

"Matter of fact we are," said Frank. "It involves the disappearance of a Japanese businessman named Satoya. Maybe you heard about it on the news broadcasts this morning."

"Indeed I did! But how can I help you?"

"For one thing," said Joe, voicing a sudden impulse, "you can tell us who that turkey was who came barreling out the door just a minute ago."

Warlord broke into a chuckle. "What happened—did he run you down?"

"He sure tried to. Call it a nasty collision. If he'd hung around for a few seconds, there might've been another collision—between one of our fists and his jaw!"

Warlord's chuckle became a hearty laugh. "Excuse

me for seeing the funny side, but that sounds just like Humber. He's one of the most pompous, arrogant louts I've ever run into."

"Who is he?" Frank inquired curiously.

"A wealthy collector."

"Of what?"

"Exotic weapons. And not only wealthy, but spoiled rotten. He thinks whenever he wants something, everyone should rush to oblige him. In my case, what he wants is a *yataghan*."

"What's that?" said Joe.

"A rather short Turkish saber with a double-curved blade," Warlord explained. "As you probably know, I use various knives and swords in my dance routine, and that *yataghan* happens to be one of them—quite a fine example of its kind, I might add. Humber wants to add it to his collection, and naturally he thinks I should sell it to him immediately at any price he cares to name."

"But you refused," Joe deduced, "so he went storming out with a bee in his ear."

"You've got the picture." Warlord grinned.

Both Hardy boys were thinking that Yvor Killian was much different from what most people might have expected a dancer to look like, especially one who had anything to do with ballet. Instead of seeming dainty or girlish, he had a square-jawed, rugged-featured face and appeared to be lithe and well muscled enough to be a fast-punching lightweight boxer. His ready grin and magnetic manner also impressed the Hardys.

"Actually, the person we meant to ask you about," said Frank, returning to the purpose of their visit, "is a man named Axel Gorky."

"Ah, yes," Warlord nodded. "The dealer in Oriental objets d'art."

"You've met him?"

"Once or twice."

"He told us last night that he came here to Bayport to call on several customers, including yourself."

Again Warlord nodded. "He wanted to show me an eighteenth-century Japanese *katana*, or long sword. In fact he called me about it this morning, but I told him I wasn't interested."

"How come," said Frank, "if I'm not too inquisitive?"

"Not at all. It just happens that I've got my heart set on another samurai sword, a really beautiful blade that I recently saw in New York. It's to be sold at auction next week at the Palmer-Glade Galleries in Manhattan, and I intend to get in the top bid!"

Frank rubbed his chin thoughtfully. "Just one thing more, sir. When we spotted this fellow Gorky at the airport, he was acting like an oddball."

The Hardys described the incident, and Frank went on, "Gorky claims he was trying to attract Mr. Satoya's attention, because he hoped Satoya might offer him a good price for the sword."

Glancing at Warlord with a frown, the older Hardy boy added, "Does that sound plausible to you? I mean, why should Gorky assume that a businessman like

Mr. Satoya would be interested in buying old samurai swords?"

"Oh yes, that strikes me as perfectly plausible," the dancer replied. "You can take my word for it, Gorky's a smart salesman. In fact I believe Satoya was planning to bid on that very sword I just mentioned—the one at the Palmer-Glade Auction Galleries."

"Well, I guess that clears Gorky, then," Frank said. "Thanks for your time and help, Mr. Killian."

"My pleasure, boys. I hope you'll come and see my troupe dance."

"We intend to," the Hardys replied.

"Good! Just phone in and tell the box office which performance you prefer. I'll see to it that tickets are reserved for you and your dates."

The boys drove off in high spirits, but their bubbling enthusiasm was somewhat deflated on arriving home. Fenton Hardy was pacing the living room floor, while their slim, pretty mother sat on the edge of a sofa trying to comfort him. From their parents' faces, Frank and Joe could tell at once that unhappy news must have struck the Hardy household.

"Something wrong, Dad?" Frank ventured cautiously.

"I've been ordered off the Satoya case!"

"What!" both boys exclaimed incredulously.

"Who did the ordering?" Joe asked.

"The U.S. government," Mr. Hardy replied. "Supposedly the FBI wants me to handle another investigation. But reading between the lines, the message is perfectly clear, namely, *get off the Satoya case!*"

"For crying out loud! They can't do that!" Frank exploded.

"They not only can, they've already done it. And I have no choice except to obey, or else risk getting my license lifted." The famed detective resumed his pacing, grim and tight-lipped.

"But won't they give you a reason?" said Joe.

"Just a lot of nonsense about government policy and more urgent priorities."

"Meaning what?"

"You figure it out. It beats me." Mr. Hardy paused and punched his fist into his other palm. His face was a study in angry frustration. "Hang it all, Satoya's disappearance reflects directly on my worth as a security expert and a private investigator. Unless I can clear up the case, my reputation may be permanently damaged. It amounts to a matter of honor! But what can I do when my hands are tied?"

"Fenton dear, you must keep calm about this," Mrs. Hardy urged soothingly. "I'm sure your reputation is well enough established to survive whatever may happen in this case. In any event, losing your cool won't help."

"You're right, Laura, as usual. All the same, it's not easy to walk away and do nothing when it's clear that all our security measures were sabotaged by someone on the inside!"

"Don't worry, Dad," Frank said. "Joe and I will do our best to solve this case."

"You bet we will!" Joe chimed in. "That's a promise!"

"I'm sure of it, sons," Mr. Hardy said proudly, putting an arm around each of the boys. "And no one could ask for a better backup team!"

Frank and Joe had little chance to discuss the case further with their father. A motorcycle meet was to be held that day as part of the Bayport Summer Festival, and Frank was scheduled to ride in an event called a Hare Scrambles. The Hardy boys had souped up a dirt bike for the race.

The brothers had a hasty lunch, then hitched up the bike trailer to their car and sped off to the scene of the meet, on the outskirts of town. Shouts of greeting went up from a group of their high school friends, who were on hand to watch the race. Among them were Chet Morton, Tony Prito, Phil Cohen, Biff Hooper and several others. The Hardys' eyes lit up when they noticed Chet's pretty sister Iola, who was Joe's favorite girl, and Callie Shaw, a brown-eyed blond whom Frank considered special.

"Looks like we've got our own cheering section," Joe chuckled.

The five-mile course had been laid out through open country in the form of a three-leafed clover and was marked with lime. The starting and finishing points were at the stem of the clover, where the judges' stand was located and most of the spectators had gathered.

Observers were stationed at checkpoints around the course.

The three cloverleaves were on rising ground, and the middle leaf extended on a fairly steep hillside. This way much of the race could be watched by viewers at the starting point.

More than a dozen participants would compete head to head. The one favored to win was riding an experimental model bike newly developed by the Road King Motorcycle Company with a revolutionary frame and suspension. But Frank and Joe had worked hard on their own bike, equipping it with a special magneto and tuned exhaust system, and they felt sure it would at least make a good showing.

One rider wore the special helmet and insignia of the Gung-Ho motorcycle gang. "Watch that guy," Biff warned Frank. "He's Lenny Boggs, the head of the gang, and I'll bet he'll pull every dirty trick in the book!"

"Thanks for telling me," Frank murmured. "I'll keep an eye open for him."

Joe, as the one-man "pit crew," gave the bike a final check. Then Frank took his place at the starting line.

A "rubberband" starting gate had been stretched across the track. At the drop of a green flag, a pin was pulled releasing the gate, and the riders took off with a roar!

Frank found himself bunched among four or five racers, which hampered his performance. As they rounded the first cloverleaf, he gradually moved up among the leaders. In doing so, he smoothly outmaneuvered and passed Lenny Boggs.

The gang leader scowled furiously and gunned his machine to top power. Bit by bit he gained ground, then tried to crowd Frank off the course.

The Hardy boy, however, refused to be scared aside, even though they were riding neck and neck. Boggs kept kicking his bike and made threatening passes trying to nudge him over. Instead, Frank concentrated on all-out speed. Once again he began to outdistance the gang leader.

"Okay, wise guy! You're asking for it!" Boggs shouted.

At this point they were passing among scattered trees, and Frank saw a broken branch hanging down from one of them. A moment later he heard a sharp crack as the gang leader reached up and yanked off the branch.

Boggs gunned his engine to full throttle. From the corner of his eye Frank saw the young hoodlum drawing abreast on his right, trying to crowd him off course, but the Hardy boy refused to let himself be unnerved.

This time, however, Boggs had a new weapon, the broken tree branch. He reached out, trying to poke it in among the spokes of Frank's front wheel!

"Knock it off!" Frank cried, turning his head. "Are you crazy?"

Not only was Boggs's trick a flagrant violation of rules and good sportsmanship—it could cause a dangerous accident!

The only way to keep the stick out of contact with his wheel was to give ground and swerve off course to the left. As Frank glanced forward again and veered his handlebars, a gasp of alarm escaped his lips. He was heading straight for a huge oak tree!

6

Flat-Out Finish

There was no time to weigh the odds. Frank had a choice of either crashing into the tree or turning back on course, which would expose him to the original danger of a shattered wheel and a possible high-speed accident!

Frank made a split-second decision. He avoided the tree, but instead of merely turning back on course, he swung hard right. He knew this meant risking a collision with Len Boggs. But by skidding his rear wheel to the left, it would also help keep the spokes out of reach of Boggs's threatening tree branch.

His move caught the gang leader utterly unprepared. Boggs yelled in fear, dropped the branch, and grabbed both handlebars in blind panic.

The next instant the two bikes collided with a loud crash! Both youths were jolted from their saddles and went sprawling on the ground!

The collision had taken place near the hairpin curve between the first and second cloverleaves, at a point where the course dipped back close to the starting point.

"That dirty rat!" gritted Joe, who had watched the incident. He started off at a run across the open field to help his brother, in case Frank had been injured. Several of the Hardys' friends followed close behind to offer whatever assistance they could.

Half a dozen members of the Gung-Ho gang also sprinted out from among the spectators and headed for the scene.

Meanwhile, other racers were veering around the two tumbled riders in order to avoid running them over. But Frank and Len Boggs were already scrambling to their feet bruised, scratched, and shaken up but otherwise uninjured.

Boggs glared with rage at the Hardy boy. "You smart punk! You're gonna pay for this!" he threatened and charged at Frank with his fists cocked.

Frank's lip curled in scorn. He did not bother to waste breath pointing out that Boggs had brought the accident on himself. Instead, his left fist swung in a whistling uppercut that connected hard with the gang leader's jaw!

Len Boggs reeled backward from the blow and landed flat on his back, too dazed to collect his wits for the next few seconds.

Without giving his foe another thought, Frank picked up his bike and hastily checked it over. The Gung-Ho's, who had seen him knock down their leader, yelled threats and abuse, and ran as fast as they could to stop him.

Frank ignored them. Swinging aboard his bike, which seemed to be in working condition, he toed the shift lever back to neutral. Then he kicked the starter, gunned his engine and roared off in pursuit of the pack!

In baffled fury, the motorcycle gang members turned to pick a fight with Joe and the Hardys' friends, who were only too willing to oblige. Phil Cohen, in fact, was already swapping punches with one of the leather-belted hoodlums.

Luckily, just then a checkpoint observer, two other race officials and a policeman reached the scene. They forced their way between the two belligerent groups, and managed to stop what might otherwise have turned into a nasty brawl.

Frank saw little of this. He was bending all his efforts toward making up for lost time. The accident with Len Boggs had been a costly interruption. Except for one lagging rider, he was now at the tail of the pack. But the second cloverleaf wound upward along the face of a steep hillside, and his souped-up dirt bike was a good climber.

Yard by yard, Frank closed the gap and regained lost ground. When he was halfway down the side of the cloverleaf, he had already nosed his way forward to the middle of the pack.

The third cloverleaf was the roughest part of the course. The terrain was not only wooded, but dotted with thick patches of brush that forced the marked-out course to zigzag crazily. The ground was bumpy and rutted and was traversed by a meandering, muddy creek which had to be crossed at two points.

Three riders had taken spills on the hillside, and two more went spinning or careening out of action on this third leg of the course.

As the first bikes in the pack came whizzing out from among the trees and into view of the spectators and judges, Joe saw that the leader was the Road King entry. But Frank was only a dozen yards behind and slowly gaining!

"He's got a chance!" Joe blurted out.

"He'll make it yet!" said Chet Morton, whose face glistened with sweat and excitement.

"Come on, Frank! *Come on!*" cheered Iola and Callie, while Tony Prito was literally gnawing his knuckles in breathless suspense.

The other riders were well back, and the race was now clearly between the Road King entry and Frank Hardy as they roared home along the final stretch of the course.

But the miracle was not to happen. As the winner's front wheel crossed the finish line, and the black-and-white checkered flag came sweeping down, Frank had not yet drawn abreast of his lone opponent!

"What a great ride!" said Joe, rushing forward to hug and congratulate his brother. "I'll bet you'd have won, if that meathead Boggs hadn't fouled you!"

"Never mind, I can't complain," said Frank, grinning happily as he pulled off his helmet.

"Not after the way you decked him with one punch." Biff chuckled. "That alone was worth a silver loving cup!"

As further consolation, Frank's girlfriend, Callie Shaw, awarded him a public kiss.

Later, after a lengthy consultation on the judges' stand, the meet referee stepped to the microphone and announced:

"Although Dave Stewart, riding the Road King entry, is the official winner, we feel that special recognition should be given to Frank Hardy. Despite a deliberate foul that slowed his time considerably, he refused to give up. As most of you saw, he plunged back into the race and, by a great display of heart and skill, he still managed to achieve a close second place!"

The announcement was greeted with cheers and thunderous applause. Frank was called to the judges' stand to be photographed with the winner and received a fresh ovation from the crowd.

Later, when the Hardys were strapping the dirt bike into the trailer, Biff joined them.

"Better keep an eye on that creep," he muttered, nudging Frank.

The older Hardy boy followed Biff's glance and saw the Gung-Ho leader talking to a tall, hawk-faced, squint-eyed man. From the dirty looks they gave the two boys, it was not hard to guess the subject of their conversation.

Frank nodded thoughtfully. "You're right, Biff. Maybe I haven't heard the last of Len Boggs."

As soon as they had showered and changed at home, Frank called the director of the Palmer-Glade Auction Galleries long distance in New York City.

"I was told by the dancer Warlord that you have an especially fine samurai sword that will soon be placed on auction," Frank began.

There was a pause. Then the director cleared his throat and replied, "Yes, that *was* correct."

Frank was puzzled. "You mean it's been removed from sale—or already sold?"

"No," came the reply. "Apparently you haven't heard the news."

"What news?"

"Our building was broken into last night and the sword you just mentioned was stolen!"

7

Cat Burglars

Frank's eyes widened on hearing this unexpected development. He flashed his brother a startled look. "Was anything else taken?" he asked.

"Luckily, no," replied the voice at the other end of the line. "It appears that whoever did it was interrupted before he or they could snatch anything more."

"I see." Frank paused a moment to consider, then said, "This may tie in with a case my brother and I are investigating. If we come to New York, could we check out the details of the break-in?"

"Of course! If you Hardys can do anything to help catch the thieves, we'll be more than happy to cooperate!"

As Frank put down the phone, Joe exclaimed, "Don't tell me the sword's been stolen?"

The older Hardy boy nodded. "You guessed it. Happened just last night."

"Boy, that sounds like more than just a coincidence, Frank! Satoya disappears—we get a lead that he may have wanted to buy a certain rare sword—and now the sword's gone too!"

"I agree, Joe. I think the burglary's worth looking into."

"Check. Let's head for New York first thing in the morning."

Frank and Joe made good time on the highway, and by ten o'clock they were parking their car in a garage just two blocks from the Palmer-Glade Auction Galleries on the Upper East Side of Manhattan.

Mr. Sanders, the gallery director, proved to be a balding, bespectacled man. He received the boys in his office and called in his security chief to help answer their questions.

"First of all, sir," Frank began, "just how valuable was this sword?"

"We expected it to bring at least twenty-five thousand dollars at auction," Sanders replied.

"Wow! That's a lot of money!" Joe murmured.

"True, but you must remember—Japanese swords have the finest blades ever produced, and many are exquisitely decorated. Today they're increasingly sought after by Western collectors."

"How was the robbery discovered?" Frank asked.

"Quite by chance," the security chief said. "A police

scout car happened along about 3:00 A.M., and the officers spotted a hole in the pane of a third-floor window. We keep a guard on the premises at night, but by the time he answered their knocks and then rushed up to the third floor to investigate, the thieves had escaped."

"You have an alarm system?" put in Joe.

"We sure do. Had the window been forced open, the alarm would have gone off. But this job was pulled by a pro—or pros. Part of the pane was cut out, using tape to keep the loose glass from falling and making any noise. Then whoever did it reached inside and disconnected the window alarm."

Frank turned back to the gallery director. "We're investigating the disappearance of that Japanese businessman you may have heard about—Takashi Satoya, the head of the Satoya Corporation. We were told he was probably planning to buy the sword that was stolen from you last night. Can you tell us if that's true?"

Sanders frowned and toyed with a bronze paperweight on his desk. "You must understand, our business requires us to be very discreet. Many customers will only deal with us because Palmer-Glade guarantees that no information will be given out about them and their bids or their purchases."

"We understand, sir. All we're trying to find out is whether there may be any connection between your burglary and what happened to Mr. Satoya."

"Let me put it this way," the gallery director said

after a brief silence. "We did receive a cabled bid from Japan."

"Any name?" Frank pursued.

"No. Just a cable address to which we were asked to send our reply. But for various reasons, I believe the offer may have come from Satoya."

"Mind telling us how much was bid?" Joe asked.

"Forty thousand dollars."

Joe whistled in awe. "But you didn't accept?"

The director shrugged. "It wouldn't have been ethical. We had already advertised the sword for auction, so we could not back out."

"Do you by any chance have a picture of the sword that we could see?" Frank queried.

"Matter of fact, I do. We had one made for our sale catalog." Mr. Sanders plucked an eight-by-ten color print from a drawer and handed it across the desk.

The Hardys studied it closely.

"Hm, the scabbard doesn't look like much," Joe remarked.

"Quite right," Mr. Sanders agreed. "The sword itself is a *tachi*, the kind that's designed to be slung from a belt, instead of merely thrust through the wearer's sash, like the kind called a *katana*. Its blade is absolutely superb. Our expert dates it as probably of sixteenth-century workmanship by a swordsmith of Mino Province. But the scabbard is what's called *shin-gunto*, or army style, just leather-covered metal, of the kind issued to military officers beginning in 1937."

"That's interesting," said Frank. "How do you explain the difference between the two?"

"It's really not all that unusual. Many officers who came from good families and owned fine old samurai swords carried them on active service—but in army scabbards, instead of the original decorated mountings." With a slight puzzled frown, the director added, "But there is one thing rather odd."

"What's that, sir?"

"When a samurai sword was converted for military wear, the owner would usually switch to a plain military hilt as well."

"How could he do that?" asked Joe.

"It's quite simple. The metal blade is held in the hilt by a peg which fits clear through the hilt and the tang, or handle end, of the blade. Remove the peg, and the hilt comes right off. But in this case, our expert couldn't figure out *how* to get it off."

"Why would he want to do that, anyhow?" said Frank.

"To examine the tang—that's where the swordsmith's signature is usually inscribed. But with this one he couldn't. However, even without knowing the maker, the fine quality of the sword was readily apparent, not only from the workmanship of the blade, but also from the hilt and the *tsuba,* or hand guard. The hilt, as you can see from the picture, is inlaid with mother-of-pearl, and the *tsuba* is embellished with intricate carving and cloisonné enamel."

"They're really beautiful," Frank agreed, then rose from his chair. "Thank you very much, Mr. Sanders, for all the information."

As Joe got up also, Frank turned to the security man. "I wonder if we could see the scene of the crime?"

"Sure thing."

The Palmer-Glade Galleries occupied a four-story building which had once been a wealthy New Yorker's town house. The merchandise was divided into departments, with Oriental *objets d'art* being grouped at the front of the third floor.

The cut windowpane had already been replaced.

"The facade of the building is quite smooth," Joe mused thoughtfully. "How do you suppose the burglar or burglars got up to the window?"

"Good question," the security man said wryly. "We still haven't figured out the answer."

"I guess they wouldn't have dared to use a ladder, even that late at night," Frank said. "How about a grappling hook and a line, to scale up the front of the building?"

"It's possible, but by heaving up the hook they would have risked making enough noise to attract the attention of the guard inside. Also, the windowsill shows no markings from a hook."

"Could a line have been dropped from the roof?" Joe asked.

The security man shook his head. "No way. The alarm system would have detected any intruder on the roof."

"And nothing else was taken but the sword?" Frank asked.

"As far as we can tell. I'm convinced they got scared off. At that time of night with the streets fairly quiet, they probably heard the scout car pull up, and they certainly would have heard the police pounding on the door. Also, an alarm *did* go off just a little later, when the guard and the cops were rushing up to the third floor to investigate."

"How come?" said Frank.

"What triggered it was the trapdoor to the roof being opened," the security man explained. "Apparently that's how the thieves got away—over the roofs of some adjoining buildings to the nearest fire escape."

The Hardy boys left the gallery soon afterward, promising to pass along any leads they might uncover.

"We still don't know for sure if the gallery heist ties in with our own case," Joe complained. "We can't even be certain Satoya did want the stolen samurai sword."

Frank nodded. "Maybe it's high time we went right to the horse's mouth."

Stopping at a public phone booth, he made a long-distance call back to Bayport, and managed to catch Mr. Oyama at the Bayport Chilton Hotel.

"Can you tell us if Mr. Satoya was planning to buy a certain samurai sword at the Palmer-Glade Galleries in New York?" Frank asked.

From the momentary silence that followed, and from Oyama's tone of voice when he finally replied,

Frank got the impression that the Japanese was surprised by his question, and especially by the fact that the Hardys had found out about the sword.

"Yes, that is correct," Oyama confirmed. "It may even have been the most important reason for his trip to America."

"How so?"

"Something must certainly have caused him to make such an unusual decision—and I am not sure that business reasons alone can explain it. Perhaps you do not realize what a drastic move this was for Mr. Satoya. Even at home in Japan, among his own people, he shuns all crowds and public appearances. Yet by flying to America, he was willing to expose himself more to the public eye than ever before."

"I understood he was coming over to discuss a business merger," Frank said.

"Yes. That is so. There is a chance the Road King Company may combine with our own motorcycle division. But if Mr. Satoya had wished, I am sure their officials would have agreed to visit Japan and talk with us, instead of Mr. Satoya coming here. For that matter," the aide added, "I believe Mr. Kawanishi and I could well have carried on the negotiations under Mr. Satoya's supervision."

"If that's so," Frank pointed out, "couldn't he have sent someone over here to buy the sword for him?"

Over the line, Frank could hear Oyama's worried

sigh. "Yes, that too seems sensible. I am afraid I do not know the answer."

Frank thanked the Japanese, then hung up and reported the conversation to his brother.

"Sure doesn't help us much," Joe grumbled.

Frank agreed and added, "We'll just have to keep scratching for leads, that's all."

New York's skyscraper office buildings were letting out their employees for lunch, and both streets and sidewalks were crowded. Everyone seemed in a hurry. Frank and Joe enjoyed watching the sea of faces all around them as they made their way back to the parking garage.

To avoid having their car jockeyed by careless attendants, the boys had purposely picked a garage which allowed them to park and lock up. But as Frank was about to insert the key in the lock, he let out a startled gasp.

"What's the matter?" Joe asked.

"Take a look! The window's been pried open, and the door's unlocked!"

The Hardys hastily checked for signs of theft and discovered that the glove compartment had been jimmied and its contents ransacked. But so far as they could determine, nothing had been taken. The trunk showed no signs of forcible entry.

Frank and Joe looked around angrily for the parking attendant on duty. The cashier's window was near the exit, well out of view of their car, but they saw a cigar-chewing man in coveralls coming down the next aisle.

"Hey!" Frank called out. "Did you see anyone monkeying with our car?"

"Nope. Why?"

"It's been broken into."

The attendant hurried over. When he saw what had happened, he scowled and snapped his fingers. "So that's it! I spotted a guy snooping around here about twenty minutes ago and chased him out. He's probably the one who did this."

"What did he look like?" Frank asked.

"Some kind of Oriental wearing shades. A tough-lookin' mug, Japanese, I think."

8

Invisible Men

Frank and Joe exchanged slightly startled looks. Both felt sure that the parking attendant had correctly spotted the guilty party.

"No doubt he was our man," Frank told the attendant.

"You want to report this to the police, or make an insurance claim? The garage is covered for any damage to a customer's car."

The older Hardy boy shook his head. "It's not worth bothering with. The only thing damaged is the glove compartment lock, which doesn't amount to much—but you ought to be more careful about keeping out intruders."

The attendant scowled again, somewhat sheepishly

this time, and removed his cigar long enough to clear his throat. "I know, I know. We try to, but there's always creeps around, waitin' to rip off anything they can get their hands on."

Joe was about to climb into the car when Frank said, "Wait a minute. We passed a drugstore on the corner, didn't we?"

"Yes. Why?"

"Let's go there before we take the car out. I've got an idea."

Leaving the garage, they walked back down the block. When they got to the drugstore, Frank led the way inside and gestured toward the soda counter. "Order me a chocolate milkshake, will you, Joe? Be right with you. There's something I want to check out first."

"Okay," said Joe, thoroughly mystified.

He saw his brother head toward a telephone booth at the rear of the store and leaf through the yellow pages of the directory.

Presently Frank returned to the counter and slid onto a stool beside Joe. "Know what kendo is?" he asked.

"Sure, it's one of the Japanese martial arts like judo or karate. Only kendo is the art of swordsmanship—right?"

"Correct. I figured there might just be a place in New York that teaches kendo, and it turns out there is. Want to go check it out? We might learn something about samurai swords that would help us on this case."

"Sure, great idea!" Joe was enthusiastic. "Even if we don't learn anything, it sounds like fun!"

After downing their milkshakes, the boys started out for the kendo studio on foot. It was on the West Side and could soon be reached by cutting across Central Park. On the way, they discussed the incident of the Japanese thug breaking into their car at the garage.

"What do you suppose he was after, Frank?" asked the younger Hardy boy.

"Maybe nothing special," Frank guessed. "Could be he was just looking for anything that might clue him in to how much we know about this whole mystery."

"Which is practically zilch at this point," Joe gloomed. "Another thing, it's not likely he just happened to spot us going into that garage or coming out. Which means he must have tailed us here all the way from Bayport."

"Right." Frank nodded. "And that tends to confirm Dad's theory about the leak in Satoya's own company."

"How do you mean?"

"If that garage creep's not American, and he's involved in the Satoya case, then he must have come here from Japan because he knew in advance about Satoya's trip. So he sure couldn't have found out through any of Dad's security arrangements over here. Someone in the Satoya Corporation must have hired him or tipped him off."

"That figures," Joe agreed.

The kendo studio was located on the ground floor of

65

a converted storefront building. Inside, there was a sound of whacks and feet thumping the floor as students in masks and padded garb practiced with bamboo swords. A calm-faced, middle-aged Japanese gentleman in cotton jacket and loose trousers came over to find out what the boys wanted. On learning that they were the sons of the famous Fenton Hardy, he smiled and bowed.

"Ah, so! My humble *dojo* is honored by your visit." He introduced himself as Ryu Shimada. The boys learned that he was attached to the Japanese Mission to the United Nations, and conducted his school in kendo as a way of introducing this ancient art to Americans.

Both Frank and Joe sensed at once that he was a man of honor who could be trusted implicitly. They told him about their work on the Satoya case. Then Frank asked his opinion about Mr. Satoya coming to the United States just to bid on a sword, despite his intense dislike of appearing in public.

"Indeed, that does not surprise me," Mr. Shimada replied. "His family belonged to the samurai, or warrior class, and in Japan it is said that the sword is the soul of the samurai. To such men, the sword is an object of veneration beyond price. Therefore he might go far to obtain a particular blade, especially if it held any family tradition."

"What about the fact that the sword had just a plain army scabbard?" Joe asked.

"Your informant was correct," said Mr. Shimada.

"Many fine antique blades were carried into battle during the war. Some were lost in combat when their owners were killed or taken prisoner. Others were sold as souvenirs during the American occupation of Japan. I am sure that many samurai swords have turned up in secondhand shops or among art dealers in this country."

But Mr. Shimada was surprised to learn that the sword still retained its original beautiful hilt that could not be removed.

"This I cannot explain," he said with a shake of his head.

To give the Hardy boys the "feel" of kendo, Mr. Shimada had them try on the equipment worn by his students. It consisted of heavily padded gauntlets, a leather apron, slatted breastplate armor and a steel-grilled helmet. The latter looked like a catcher's mask and was worn over a towel to keep perspiration from running down in the fencer's eyes.

The boys were required to kneel while the armor was being tied on. This was an important part of *reigi*, the discipline or etiquette of kendo.

"The purpose of kendo, you see, is not merely to train a fierce fighting man," Mr. Shimada said, then tapped his head and chest. "More important is its effect on mind and heart."

By teaching the student to overcome the "Four Poisons of Kendo"—fear, doubt, surprise and confusion—it also helped to develop character and self-control.

"The training that your distinguished father is giving you in the art of detection," he added, "has probably much the same effect."

Frank and Joe tried some of the basic attacks and parries of kendo, using *shinai,* or bamboo practice swords. They were shown how to leap forward and swing the sword in a fierce downward chop, then skip backward out of range, and also how to crouch and slash.

The explosive *kiai,* or shouting, that accompanied these blows was meant to put spirit into the swordsman and shock his opponent off balance.

"Like the rebel yell the Confederates used during the Civil War," Joe chuckled.

Both boys felt they had been through a real workout when they finally shucked their armor. Afterward, they listened with keen interest as Mr. Shimada and his pupils discussed other Japanese martial arts, such as kyudo or archery, judo, karate and aikido—as well as special weapons such as the *naginata* or curved-bladed spear, the *bo* stave and the iron fan.

Frank and Joe pricked up their ears at the mention of a special class of warriors called *ninja,* who were experts at *ninjutsu*—the art of remaining invisible. They dressed all in black, and in olden times were often used as spies.

"Do *ninja* still exist?" Frank asked.

"Oh, yes," the kendo master replied. "But their art was always so secret that no one can be sure how much of it was real and how much just hearsay. Some actually think *ninjutsu* involved magic. Others say it depended on trickery or hypnosis."

As the Hardys started back to the parking garage, Frank said, "Remember that sneak in black we thought we saw outside Pete Ogden's house?"

"I'll say I do!" Joe exclaimed. "And you're probably wondering the same thing I am—namely, if he could have been a *ninja*."

"Right now I'm ready to believe almost anything," Frank said, "including the fact that someone's tailing us."

Joe shot his brother a startled look. "Are you serious?"

"You bet I am! Don't look now, but keep your eyes and ears open, Joe."

The boys entered Central Park just south of the American Museum of Natural History. As they crossed a wooden bridge, they paused to look down at the water of the lake. Joe used the opportunity to steal a cautious glance behind them.

"Yes. I see the guy," he muttered. "Looks Oriental, all right—and he's wearing dark glasses, like the crook who broke into our car!"

Beyond the bridge, the Hardys turned onto a paved walk which wound through the park. They discussed a plan of action as they strolled along. A dirt path led off among some craggy rocks. Frank and Joe took this path, and as it turned sharply through a sort of rocky gorge, they scrambled hastily up the slope and flung themselves flat.

Moments later they heard footsteps approaching, and their Oriental shadow came into view. He had crew-cut dark hair and wore a loud checked sports coat.

"*Now!*" hissed Frank, and the two boys leaped down at him! Each grabbed one of his arms.

"Now, mister," Frank gritted, "you're going to tell us why you're following us!"

Instead of answering, their opponent fought furiously. He seemed as strong as a bull and was clearly adept at unarmed combat. Twisting and turning, he wrested his arms free, using them like flails.

Joe thought he saw an opening and swung at the man with a hard right hook. But the man was no longer there. Joe's fist merely sailed past his jaw and hit Frank on the side of the head, sending him sprawling backward!

An instant later Joe himself caught a sword-hand jab in the pit of the stomach. As he crumpled, gasping for breath, he saw the Oriental flee from the gorge!

9

Lurking Shadows

Frank was the first to recover. Scrambling to his feet, he dashed after their unknown enemy. But the Oriental had a long head start. By the time Joe rejoined his brother, the man was already out of sight. He was either lost from view among the trees and rocks, or else had managed to blend in among other park strollers and loungers without attracting attention.

"Oh, rats!" Frank fumed. "We had the guy in our clutches and let him go! He might've given us a clue to whatever happened to Mr. Satoya!"

"Sorry I decked you," Joe apologized. "That punch was meant for our attacker."

"It wasn't your fault. He was one tough cookie. At least we'll be able to identify him if we ever see him again. Did you notice his tattoos?"

"I'll say I did! Oriental dragons and evil spirits sticking out of both sleeves; they probably run clear up his arms. And did you notice his little fingers?"

Frank nodded grimly. "You mean what's left of them. They were both missing the top joints!"

Back home in Bayport that evening, the boys described the attacker to their father. From Fenton Hardy's expression, it was clear that he recognized the description at once.

"The fellow must have been a *Yakuza!*" he declared.

"What's that?" Joe queried.

"A Japanese gangster. They're almost a separate caste over there. The crew cut and dark glasses and loud clothes sound typical. So do the tattoos and especially the amputated finger joints."

"How come, Dad?"

"It's a ritual," Mr. Hardy explained. "Whenever a gang member does something wrong in the eyes of his leader, he is required to cut off a finger joint. This proves that he is still loyal and shows that he regrets his mistake."

The younger Hardy boy shuddered. "Sounds sick to me!"

"I warned you two! You were asking for trouble when you went poking around New York looking for bloodthirsty Oriental criminals!" Gertrude Hardy scolded. She was hovering within hearing distance as she finished setting the dinner table.

"If you mean the art gallery thieves, Aunt Gertrude,

there's no way of telling whether or not they were Orientals," Frank pointed out.

The tall, thin woman sniffed scornfully. "Who else would want to steal a Japanese sword?"

"Quite a few crooks, I imagine, if they knew it was worth twenty-five thousand dollars."

"Don't argue with me, young man! Just come to dinner!" Miss Hardy disappeared into the kitchen to bring out the roast, muttering darkly, "Tattooed gangsters! Chopped-off finger joints! Next thing we'll be getting poisoned fortune cookies in the mail!"

After dinner, Frank and Joe found time to glance through the evening paper. Joe had the front section, which carried stories about Takashi Satoya's baffling disappearance, and also the break-in theft of the samurai sword from the Palmer-Glade Auction Galleries.

"Hey, get a load of this!" Joe muttered to his brother.

"What?" said Frank, scarcely looking up from the comics page.

"Remember that klutz who bumped into us when we went to see Warlord?"

"Humber? Sure, what about him?"

"There's an interview with him in the paper."

Frank put down the comics page with an expression of interest. "What's he got to say?"

"He thinks there may be a connection between Satoya disappearing and the gallery theft—*because the stolen sword belonged to the Satoya family!*"

"Hey! Let's see that!" Frank exclaimed, springing up

from the sofa. Taking the newspaper from his brother, he ran his eyes hastily over the story that Joe was pointing to.

Apparently Humber had been interviewed as an expert on swords because of his own collection of exotic weapons.

"I would not care to speculate on why the sword was stolen, or who may have engineered the theft," he was quoted as saying, "but the timing and coincidence are certainly interesting!"

"Boy, Humber's taking a chance, making a crack like that!" Frank remarked thoughtfully.

"You said it," Joe agreed. "Almost sounds as if he's accusing Satoya. The Satoya Corporation might decide to sue Big Mouth!"

"He's probably banking on Satoya being too publicity shy to take him to court. Or maybe he just likes to hear himself talk, and let his mouth run away with him."

From the pompous tone of the interview, Humber did indeed sound as if he enjoyed basking in the limelight, however briefly or unimportantly.

"We still ought to check this out," Frank said soberly as he handed back the paper to his brother.

"Right." Joe nodded. "If he knows something we don't know, the sooner we find out the better!"

Mr. Hardy had gone out again after dinner to resume his own investigative work, so the boys were unable to ask his advice. Frank, therefore, took the most direct approach. He called the wealthy collector for an appointment.

"Hm, haven't I heard your name before?" Dobert Humber said.

"Our father's a private investigator," Frank replied. "He's quite well known."

"Oh yes. And you and your brother run some kind of boyish detective service, I believe."

"That's right. We're trying to find out what happened to Mr. Satoya. That's why we'd like to talk to you about that stolen sword."

"I see. Well, if I can be of any help, I shall be glad to spare you a few minutes. It's quite possible my knowledge and expertise may shed some light on the mystery."

Joe flashed his brother a questioning glance as Frank hung up the phone a few seconds later.

"Well?"

"He'll see us tonight," Frank said with a grimace. "Sounds like a real fathead!"

The boys drove out to see Humber, who lived in a beautiful wooded area outside of town. His home, built of gray stone, looked like a huge old English manor house. As they started up to the front door after parking their car, Frank suddenly put a hand on his brother's right arm.

Joe guessed at once that Frank had noticed something unusual. "What is it?" he murmured.

"Left side of the house. Thought I saw a movement in the shadows."

Without any hasty action that might telegraph their intentions, Joe casually returned to the car and got a flashlight. Then he and Frank darted in opposite directions, trying to cut off the intruder's escape. But the flashlight beam failed to reveal any lurking figures.

"Maybe I was seeing things again," Frank fretted.

"Maybe and maybe not. Never hurts to check."

A butler admitted the boys to the drawing room where Humber was waiting. If their host recognized the Hardys as the two youths he had bumped into at Bayshore College, he gave no sign. Instead, he offered them refreshments and insisted on showing them his collection of rare weapons.

Most of them were displayed in glass cases or hung on the walls of his study. Frank and Joe were fascinated as Humber pointed out his treasures. Among them were an ancient Saxon war axe dating back before the Norman Conquest of England, a knobkerry or African throwing club, a two-bladed scissors dagger from the Middle East, and a *katar* or punch dagger from India. The latter had a handle with twin crossbars, which the user could hold in order to jab an enemy, the same way a boxer punches with his fist.

"And this curious weapon also comes from India," said Humber, holding up a small but vicious-looking device. "These curved steel blades are called 'tiger claws.'"

The claws were attached to a steel bar with a little ring at each end. Humber showed the boys how the wearer could slip his first and little fingers through these rings in order to slash an opponent.

"Wow!" Joe muttered. "I'd hate to tangle with anyone wearing *those!*"

"A very nasty weapon," Humber agreed. "I'm told these were often used sneakily, to attack an enemy off guard."

He seemed pleased by the boys' interest in his collection and answered all their questions. Frank maneuvered the conversation around to the reason for their visit.

"We're wondering how you knew that stolen samurai sword belonged to Mr. Satoya's family," he probed.

Their host said he had been told so. "The fact wasn't mentioned in the sale catalog for the auction, but I'm a valued customer of the Palmer-Glade Galleries," Humber said smugly. "I daresay that's why their Oriental expert confided the information to me."

Frank threw a glance at Joe. Both boys had the same idea. No doubt this explained why the gallery director believed the anonymous Japanese offer to buy the sword might have come from Satoya. But he had not revealed his reasons to the boys in order to protect his gallery's reputation for being discreet about its customers' affairs.

"Matter of fact, that dancer Warlord told us Mr. Satoya was probably interested in purchasing the sword," Joe said. "I wonder how *he* found out?"

"Hm! Good question," Humber sniffed disdainfully. "In my opinion that Warlord fellow's not to be trusted—especially about anything connected with the Satoya Corporation."

Frank frowned alertly. "Why not, sir?"

"Because I've reason to believe he's involved in a nasty feud with the company."

"What sort of feud, Mr. Humber?" Joe asked.

Their host shrugged as if he found the subject too unpleasant to talk about. "It started when Warlord was over in Japan. There was trouble of some kind—actual physical violence, or so I've heard. But I wouldn't know the details."

Again the Hardys exchanged thoughtful looks.

As they were leaving, Humber said, "By the way, I may need some detective work done myself one of these days."

Frank politely inquired the reason.

"Because I suspect thieves may have their eye on my collection of weapons," Humber replied. "Possibly professional burglars."

"Do you have any definite grounds for your suspicions?" Frank persisted.

"Indeed I do, though you may think I'm worrying about shadows. This evening at twilight, just before it got dark, I'm sure I saw someone spying on the house. It was a man dressed all in black!"

10

Trouble in Tokyo

Joe was about to blurt out that Frank, too, had glimpsed a dark figure, as a result of which they had made a hasty search for any lurking spy just before ringing the doorbell. But he stifled his remark at a slight frown from his brother.

"If it happens again, Mr. Humber, please give us a call," Frank said. "We'll come right over and try to trap whoever's watching your house."

"Thanks! I'll certainly do that." Humber sounded genuinely grateful for the offer of help.

As the boys drove away, Frank explained, "No sense worrying the guy—that's why I signaled you not to mention what we saw. Or what *I* saw, anyhow."

"Guess you're right," Joe agreed. "At least we know it

wasn't your imagination." He added after a pause, "You think it was a *ninja?*"

Frank nodded thoughtfully. "It's sure beginning to look that way. What do you make of that trouble Humber mentioned, between Warlord and the Satoya Corporation?"

"Sounded to me like he's peeved at Warlord, so he's raking up some old business to make him look bad."

"I got the same impression. On the other hand, if Warlord really does have a grudge against the company, I'd like to know more about it."

"Same here. Maybe we ought to have another talk with Warlord."

It was not yet 9:30, so the Hardys felt there might still be a chance of seeing the dancer before he retired. Frank pulled into a gas station. Leaving Joe to deal with the attendant, he dialed the number of Bayshore College on the pay telephone inside and asked for Warlord's extension in the dance troupe's quarters on campus.

Another member of the troupe answered. "Yvor's not here right now," he said, using Warlord's given name. "May I help you?"

Frank told the dancer who was calling and said, "My brother and I would like to ask him about something that happened when he was in Japan."

"That must've been before he formed our troupe, so I wouldn't know about it, myself," the dancer replied. "But look, you're the fellows who were here before, aren't you, investigating the disappearance of that Japanese businessman?"

"That's right."

"Well, the campus is still lit up, and things seem pretty lively around here. Yvor should be back soon— so if you want to take a chance and come on over, I imagine he'll see you."

"Great! Thanks," Frank said. "We'll be there in about fifteen or twenty minutes."

The Hardys drove to Bayshore. With many students on vacation during the summer term, two of the dormitories were empty, and the dance troupe had been assigned rooms in one of them. But the boys were in for an unpleasant surprise.

When they knocked on Warlord's door, it was opened by another member of the troupe. From his look of instant recognition, Frank guessed that this must be the person he had talked to on the phone.

"We're Frank and Joe Hardy," he said. "We've come to—"

"I know—I know who you are," the dancer interrupted hastily, with an embarrassed expression on his face. "But I'm not too sure th—"

He was pushed aside before he could finish speaking, and Warlord himself appeared in the doorway, looking furious.

"I have nothing to say to you two!" he exclaimed. "So kindly leave!"

The Hardys stared in astonishment. Unlike his

friendly manner that morning, the dance star was red-faced with anger.

"What're you upset about?" Frank asked in a reasonable tone, hoping to calm him down. "All we want to do is ask you a few qu—"

But Warlord cut him short and growled, "Get out!" and slammed the door in their faces!

The Hardys returned somewhat glumly to their car.

"Boy, I sure wasn't expecting anything like that," Joe remarked.

"Neither was I," Frank concurred. "Whatever happened in Japan must still be a mighty sore point with him. Maybe Humber was right."

When the boys arrived back at the Hardys' house on Elm Street, they found their father home again. They learned that he had gone to the airport to confer with an FBI official, who had flown from Washington expressly to brief him on his new assignment.

"What do they want you to do, Dad?" Joe asked. "I mean if it's not too secret to tell us."

"Actually it may well be connected with the Satoya case," Fenton Hardy replied. "The Road King Motorcycle Company has received certain threats."

"There's a chance they may merge with the motorcycle division of the Satoya Corporation," Frank put in. "That's what Mr. Satoya came over to discuss."

Mr. Hardy nodded. "Right—and that's what the threats are all about. Road King's been warned to forget the merger, or they'll regret it."

"Any leads to go on, Dad?"

"Not really—just suspicions. I have a hunch the threats may have come from another Japanese firm, Gorobei Motors. They'd like to take over the Road King company themselves. In fact they've already made an offer. If my suspicions are correct, I may have to fly to Japan to prove them, but so far I'm not sure."

After hearing about the unpleasant incident with Warlord, Mr. Hardy offered to cable the Japanese police for information. "I know several of the top police officials in Tokyo," he said. "I've even handled a few investigations for them. If Warlord was ever in trouble over there, I'm sure they could check out the facts."

"Great! Thanks, Dad," his sons responded.

Next morning, Frank and Joe went to the Bayport Chilton Hotel to see Takashi Satoya's two senior aides. They noticed his rugged-looking, poker-faced chauffeur sitting in the lobby. He returned their nods politely.

"Looks like he's keeping an eye out for trouble himself," Joe remarked in a low voice as they headed for an elevator.

"Yes, backing up the regular security guards," Frank agreed. "And if any trouble does come up, he sure looks as if he could handle it."

Mr. Kawanishi and Mr. Oyama received them in the sitting room of the company's hotel suite.

"We're wondering if you could tell us anything about

an American dancer called Warlord," Frank began. "It happens he's in Bayport to perform, and we were told he once had trouble with the Satoya Corporation when he was in Japan."

Satoya's aides regarded the Hardy boys with fresh respect.

"You two young men do, indeed, carry out thorough investigations," Mr. Kawanishi said. "And what you say is correct. I recall our company having trouble of some kind with the dancer called Warlord, although it happened several years ago."

Mr. Oyama explained, "He had a fight with one of our employees—a grudge fight, I believe, in which our employee was seriously injured and had to go to the hospital. As you may know, in Japan, companies take a keen interest in the private lives of their workers, as well as in how they perform their jobs. Therefore, the Satoya Corporation took legal action against Warlord, on behalf of our injured worker."

As a result, he went on, the dancer had been forced to leave Japan. However, all this had been handled by company lawyers, and neither Mr. Oyama nor Mr. Kawanishi knew any of the details. Nor, up until now, at least, had they considered it very important.

"Are you suggesting that Warlord may know something about our revered employer's disappearance?" Kawanishi inquired.

"It's one possibility we wanted to look into," said Frank. "We'd also like to know a little more about this samurai sword that was stolen in New York. Mr. Oyama told me on the phone that the sword may have been Mr. Satoya's main reason for coming to America."

Both aides nodded seriously as though they had discussed the matter between them, following Frank's phone call.

"Our employer wore the sword as a young officer during World War II," Oyama related, "but he lost it when he was taken prisoner by your soldiers, sometime before Japan surrendered. Apparently the sword was 'liberated,' as the saying goes, by a GI. At any rate, it disappeared. Perhaps you know how much a Japanese samurai values his blade?"

"We've been told," said Frank.

"This one was especially treasured because it had belonged to the Satoya family for many generations," Mr. Kawanishi added. "For that reason, our employer has had agents looking for it all over the world, feeling that one day whoever took it might decide to sell it for money."

"And events proved him right," said Mr. Oyama. "He was delighted when the sword turned up for sale at the Palmer-Glade Galleries. He was able to identify it from their sale catalog. But, alas, I fear the news of its theft may come as a very unpleasant blow to him—that is, assuming Mr. Satoya himself is still alive and safe."

"You think he disappeared of his own accord?" Joe asked shrewdly.

Once again, the Hardys saw a troubled glance pass between the two aides.

"I must confess we do think so," Mr. Kawanishi admitted, "even though we are at a loss to explain how or why it happened."

"If you're right, his chauffeur must have been in on it," Frank pointed out.

Both aides agreed. "But there is no hope of learning anything from him," said Oyama.

"Why not, sir?"

"Because he is fanatically loyal to his master. You see, he has a small daughter, who was born with a heart defect. Mr. Satoya had her flown to a hospital in Texas and paid for an expensive operation that saved her life. Now that fellow would die before he would betray anything which his master wished to keep secret."

On a sudden impulse, Frank decided to phone Warlord from the hotel lobby. As he had hoped, the dancer accepted his call.

"We've found out about the fight you had with a Satoya worker, and how you were forced to leave Japan," Frank said. "We'd like to hear your side of it, just out of fairness."

There was a brief silence. Then Warlord said, "Okay, you win. Come on over to the college and I'll tell you the whole story."

11

A Crooked Offer

"We'll be right over," Frank promised and hung up.

Joe was excited when he heard the news. "Maybe something'll break now!"

"Maybe. But we'd better not get our hopes too high. This may turn into another blind alley."

The boys sped to Bayshore College. After parking their car in the student lot, they found Yvor Killian and his troupe practicing their numbers in the gymnasium again.

The dancer's manner was somewhat embarrassed as he greeted the Hardys.

"Come over and sit down, please, where we can talk in private," he said, gesturing toward some folding chairs in one corner of the gym.

When they were all seated, Killian began, "About three years ago, before I formed my present troupe, I studied the martial arts in Japan."

"How come?" Joe asked.

"Because I thought they might add an important touch to the kind of dance spectacle I was interested in creating. I enjoyed learning the Japanese fighting skills and the way they were taught, partly because it was all so different from our American self-defense sports like boxing, for example. But there was one student, named Noguchi, with whom I never got along. He hated me— maybe because his father had been killed fighting the Americans during the war."

Killian said the bad feelings between them erupted one day during a practice match. Noguchi had refused to "pull" his blows. This enraged Killian. They were soon fighting in deadly earnest, and before their instructor could stop them, Killian hit his opponent with a karate chop, seriously injuring him.

The dancer's head drooped for a moment and his face took on a bleak expression as he recalled the unpleasant situation.

"I instantly regretted it," he went on, "and I tried to make amends by visiting Noguchi at the hospital and apologizing. But by then the damage was done. Noguchi worked for the Satoya Corporation, and their company lawyers pressed charges against me with the police. As a result, I was asked to leave the country."

"Tough break," Frank sympathized.

Warlord shrugged. "Just one of those things, I guess. Noguchi recovered, but I still feel guilty about what happened, so I've tried to forget the whole business. If the news ever came out, it probably wouldn't do my career any good, either."

"Don't worry, it's not going to leak out through us," said Joe.

"No, I'm sure of that—now. But at the time I got your call and heard what you wanted to see me about, I guess I lost my head. I thought you were going to drag up that old scandal and try to pin something on me. Sorry about that."

"Forget it," Frank said. "But we do have another question . . ."

"Shoot."

"You told us you thought Satoya intended to bid on that sword at the Palmer-Glade Auction Galleries, and it turns out you were right. How did you know?"

"That sword's been stolen, by the way," Joe added.

Warlord nodded. "So I've heard. Well, I felt Satoya would be interested in it, because when I looked at the blade while it was on display, I noticed the name *Satoya* inscribed on it. You see, while I was in Japan, I learned to read Japanese characters. And when you mentioned that dealer, Gorky, trying to sell him a samurai sword, it just seemed likely he'd be more interested in buying one that belonged to his own family." The dancer rose from his chair and began to pace the floor. His manner seemed vaguely uncomfortable.

"There's something else I'd better tell you," he said after a few moments.

"We're listening," Frank said.

"Last night I had an anonymous phone call."

"What about?" Joe asked.

"That samurai sword. Apparently the person who called was the thief who stole it from the auction gallery—or maybe a fence. He offered to sell me the sword—for ten thousand dollars."

Warlord's startling news caught the Hardys by surprise. They stared at him, wide-eyed.

"How did you handle it?" Frank asked.

Warlord ran his fingers nervously through his mane of long black hair. "To tell the truth I didn't know *what* to say. He only gave me a few moments to make up my mind, and I was afraid if I said no, that would be the last I'd hear from him. So I said I'd accept, and he named a time and place to complete the deal."

"You bring the money, and he'd hand over the sword?"

"Right."

"When and where is this supposed to take place?"

"Midnight tonight at Seaview Park."

"Did you intend to go through with it?" Joe put in.

The dancer shrugged helplessly. "I don't know *what* I intended. The whole thing's been on my mind ever since I got the call. Guess that's why I was glad to hear from you fellows again—so you could advise me."

"If you buy stolen goods, that makes you as guilty as the thief," Frank pointed out.

"I realize that. But I wasn't planning on just keeping the sword and saying nothing. It wouldn't be any use to me, anyhow, if I had to keep it hidden. I thought if I returned it to the auction gallery, they might be willing to sell it to me for a bargain price—I mean, to make up for the ransom money I'd already paid out."

"You might find a lot of people would suspect you were the guy who swiped it in the first place," Joe remarked dryly.

From the dismayed look on Warlord's face, the boys could see that this possibility hadn't even occurred to him. "So what choice do I have at this point?" Killian asked the Hardys.

"Use the payoff meeting as a chance to catch the thieves," Frank shot back.

"They warned me I'd regret it if I tipped off the police—and not just myself, my whole dance troupe!"

"You agreed not to tell the police?"

"The caller made me swear it before he named the time and place for the exchange."

"Leave it to us," said Joe after a questioning glance at his brother, who responded with a nod. "That way you'll be keeping your word, and Frank and I will try to set up a trap on our own."

Warlord's expression showed relief at getting out of his dilemma, and he readily agreed to the Hardys' proposal.

"One more thing," said Frank. "How would the thief or thieves have known *you* might be interested in buying that stolen sword?"

"The gallery's public relations man had a publicity photo taken of me examining the sword," Killian replied. "It turned up in a couple of newspapers, and the caption under the picture said I planned to bid on the sword when it was auctioned."

"That would explain it, all right," Frank agreed.

"Besides," Warlord added, "everyone who's seen my show knows that I use swords and knives in my dance act—and each one's an authentic example of its kind."

As the Hardys returned to their car in the parking lot, Frank murmured, "Oh, oh! Something must be up!"

A red light was flashing on their instrument panel. Frank switched on the specially licensed transceiver mounted under their dashboard.

"H-1 here," he said into the hand mike.

"G calling!"

Something in the tone of the woman's voice as it came over the speaker struck a note of alarm in the hearts of both Hardy boys.

"What's wrong, Aunt Gertrude?" Frank asked.

"Sam Radley's been hurt!" she reported. "I just had a call from Shoreham. He was found unconscious in the street there—with a head wound!"

12

A Meeting at Midnight

"Oh, that's terrible news!" Frank exclaimed with an anxious glance at Joe. "Where is Sam now?"

"They've taken him to Shoreham Hospital," Miss Hardy replied. "The police recognized him as your father's top aide, so they called here. But so far I haven't been able to reach Fenton and give him the bad news. That's why I called you boys."

"Good! I'm glad you let us know, Aunty. Joe and I'll drive to the hospital right now and see how Sam is. Over and out!"

Frank switched off the set and hung up the mike. Then he gunned the engine and maneuvered smoothly and swiftly out of the parking lot. Soon they were pressing the speed limit over the Shore Road, en route to the nearby town of Shoreham.

"Do you suppose this is connected to the Satoya case?" Joe asked his brother.

"I don't know. I'm not sure what kind of assignment Dad had him working on."

At the hospital they were directed to the emergency room. Sam Radley had already regained consciousness. The boys found him sitting up on the examining table while a doctor bandaged his head.

"Wow! What a relief!" Frank exclaimed. "We weren't sure what had happened, or how seriously you were hurt!"

Joe added, "What did happen, Sam?"

"Got conked." The detective grinned wryly. "Fortunately I seem to have a hard head."

Frank gave the medic a questioning glance. "How is he, Doctor?"

"Nothing too serious, apparently. Just a bruise and a slight scalp laceration. Bit swollen now, but that'll be down by tomorrow morning. However, I want him to stay here at the hospital overnight, to make sure he's suffered no concussion."

The doctor allowed the Hardys to talk to Sam Radley for a few minutes before he was taken to one of the hospital wards.

"Any idea who hit you, Sam?" Frank inquired.

"No name, if that's what you mean—but I've got a general idea."

Although Radley was the only investigator who worked regularly for Fenton Hardy, there were other operatives whom the sleuth employed from time to time as the need arose. Sam told the boys that their father had asked all his associates to keep their eyes open for any possible *Yakuza*, or Japanese gangsters, in the area.

"I spotted a guy here in Shoreham with all the ear-marks," the private detective went on. "Tattooed arms, flashy clothes, amputated finger joints, the works. So I started tailing him."

"Where'd he go?" Joe asked eagerly.

"To a cafe down on the waterfront. And he met a man there, an American, from the looks of him, anyhow." Sam paused for a moment, his brow creasing in a thoughtful frown.

"Did you recognize him?" Frank prompted.

"I don't know. And that bothers me a bit." Sam hesitated, still frowning. "He looked familiar, but I can't place him. Anyhow, the two of them gabbed for a while, then the *Yakuza* got up and left. And I followed him—which turned out to be a mistake."

"How do you mean?"

"I figure he may have suspected he was being shadowed, so he told the American to keep watch. Or maybe the American saw me follow him out of the cafe, and took action on his own hook, or tipped off one of the *Yakuza*'s pals. Whichever it was, the Japanese led me down a narrow street near the wharves. Next thing I knew someone jumped me from behind!"

"Did you get a look at the person who attacked you?" put in Joe.

"Nope." Sam Radley shook his head in disgust. "Not even out of the corner of my eye. He just grabbed my coat long enough to slow me down, then let me have it with a blackjack, or whatever it was he hit me with. All I remember after that is waking up here in the hospital emergency room."

Sam speculated that his assailant might have been hiding in a doorway as he passed.

Frank and Joe started back to Bayport in a somewhat grim mood. Both were disturbed over the attack on Sam Radley. Partly to get their minds off the subject, Joe switched on the radio and tuned in the police frequency.

The first calls were routine and not very interesting. Then the boys heard the dispatcher say, "Car Seven, proceed to 119 Ardmore Avenue, corner of Dean Street. Investigate report of an escaped monkey."

"Escaped monkey?" The man responding from the scout car sounded startled.

"That's right. It got loose from a pet shop."

There was a burst of static and a blurred mutter of voices. Then the man exclaimed, "That must have been what we saw!"

"What do you mean 'what you saw'?" the dispatcher queried irritably.

"A man running down the street with a monkey on his head!"

"What?"

"We saw this guy running down the street with a monkey on his head," the officer repeated. "He did

97

look kind of excited, and we wondered what was going on, but. . . ."

"For crying out loud!" the dispatcher sounded angry. "What did you *think* was going on—that the monkey was prospecting for coconuts?"

"No. We figured the animal was the fellow's pet, and they were just having fun, or else he was taking it out for exercise, something like that."

"Listen! Next time you see someone with a monkey on his head, *find out* what's going on, understand? Now get moving and round up the critter before it attacks someone else!"

"Roger."

Frank and Joe were shaking with laughter as they neared the outskirts of Bayport. Before driving to their house on Elm Street, they stopped off at the Morton farm, where they found their chubby friend, Chet, squaring off against lanky Biff Hooper in the barnyard.

"What's this? A grudge match?" Frank asked, noting Chet's intense scowl of concentration. Although he spoke half jokingly, he was ready to step between the two youths instantly if the fight turned out to be real.

"No, haven't you heard?" Biff asked, not taking his eyes off his pudgy opponent.

"Heard what?" Joe asked.

"Chet's taking up the martial arts," Biff explained. "He's showing me the fine points of karate or kung fu or wing ding or something."

"Think I'm kidding, huh?" Chet retorted. "Well,

watch this, wise guy! It's a combination. First a feint, then a move backward to draw you off balance, then a series of blows to finish you off, using a mixture of two different Oriental fighting styles. *On guard!*"

Chet took a couple of quick, shuffling dance steps and flailed out with both arms before leaping backward out of range. The next instant Biff's long left snaked out in a fast jab, and their plump chum landed flat on his back!

"No fair!" Chet grumbled loudly as he scrabbled back up on his feet. "You weren't supposed to get that close!"

"How do I know what I'm supposed to do?" Biff retorted. "I'm just defending myself."

"Then do it right, meatball!"

"Meatball, eh? Look who's talking!"

The Hardys, who had a hard time to keep from howling with laughter, hastily intervened before the exhibition could, indeed, turn into a grudge match.

"Listen, you guys!" Frank said. "How'd you like a chance to show off your fighting styles tonight?"

"What's up?" Biff asked.

"A ransom stakeout. Joe and I are going to try and catch a thief. If he makes a run for it, we may need help in stopping and subduing him."

The Hardys explained about the anonymous call Warlord had received, offering to sell him the stolen samurai sword, and the meeting that had been set up at Seaview Park.

"Count me in!" Chet exclaimed. "Boy, this'll really

give me a chance to show you how they do it in the Orient. If this guy makes one false move, I'll have him hollering uncle so fast that his head'll swim."

"Great! But don't take any chances," Frank cautioned. "If the man's armed, or comes with pals who may be armed, none of us makes any move. Just watch for a signal from me."

Biff was as eager as Chet to lend a hand in the nocturnal trap baiting.

That night, after a final phone check with Warlord to coordinate their movements, the Hardys picked up Chet and Biff in their car. Then, shortly after 10:30, the boys headed down Ardmore Avenue. It connected with a cinder road that wound through the full length of Seaview Park.

The park itself was a pleasant wooded stretch, bordered on one side by the coastal highway and on the other by the water. Officially it closed at eleven every night, but there was no gate or roadblock. Youngsters and dating couples often sneaked in later by moonlight or stayed after the official closing time.

Frank, Joe and their two friends parked the Hardys' yellow car out of sight among some trees. Then they found a comfortable spot where they could sprawl and listen to music on Biff's transistor radio or tell yarns to pass the time.

At about a quarter to twelve, they took up hiding places around the point where the meeting had been set up. It was a short dirt turnoff which ended in a parking site near two or three picnic tables.

Shortly before midnight, they heard the low hum of a car engine and saw a glow of headlights. They were doused as a sleek white car pulled to a stop on the parking site.

"Warlord," Joe hissed to his brother, who was crouched in a crevice between two rocks.

Soon afterward, the *putput* of a motorboat drifted over the water. It died away abruptly, as the engine was shut off, but moments later the boat could be heard pulling alongside the shore embankment. Apparently its operator had allowed the craft to coast toward the park.

At that moment there was a loud commotion from a tree a dozen yards away, where the Hardys' chubby friend was perched among the branches.

"Something's wrong with Chet!" Frank exclaimed.

13

Masked Riders

In the shadowy moonlight, the Hardys could clearly see the tree in which Chet was hiding. Its branches were swaying violently.

"What is going on?" Joe gasped.

"Help!" their fat chum yelled in fright.

Before either of the Hardys could respond, there was an explosive *crack* as one of the tree limbs snapped under its heavy load. The next instant, Chet tumbled down into view!

Frank and Joe hesitated no longer. They knew their stakeout would be ruined, but they ran to help their friend. Warlord was jumping out of his car at the same time.

"Chet!" Frank cried. "Are you all right?"

Their roly-poly pal struggled painfully to his feet and dusted off the seat of his pants. "D-D-Don't ask me!" he stuttered. "I was attacked by some wild animal up in the tree!"

"Wild animal?" Joe gaped at Chet, not quite sure he was serious.

"You heard me!" Chet retorted. "Boy, it was really savage! Is my face all clawed up?"

"Not a scratch as far as I can see!" Joe declared.

"Well, stop staring at me as if I were nuts! I'm telling you th—"

Whatever Chet was about to tell his baffled audience was drowned out by the sudden roar of a motorboat engine being revved into action.

At the same instant something plopped out of the tree onto Chet's head. *It was a live monkey!*

Chet screeched in fright and hopped about, clutching wildly at his excited furry rider!

Frank and Joe did not wait to watch the uproarious spectacle. Half amused, half furious at the wreckage of their carefully laid plans, they turned and darted down the park's wooded slope toward the water's edge.

Too late! The motorboat they had heard was already speeding off into the darkness. Its pilot cautiously hugged the shadow of the hillside in order to avoid being silhouetted in the moonlight. The Hardys could not even tell whether the boat held more than one occupant.

"Great!" Frank fumed. "So much for our stakeout!"

"Not only didn't we catch the thief," Joe added in disgust, "we didn't even get the sword back!"

"Never mind. Maybe the whole thing was a con job anyhow, just to help someone get his hands on ten thousand dollars."

"Guess you're right." Joe did his best to emulate his brother's example and swallow his disappointment. "Blowing our stacks won't do us any good."

The Hardys headed back up the slope toward the meeting place. Biff had joined forces with Warlord to try and pry the chattering monkey loose from its perch on Chet's head.

A passing policeman, who had heard the noise, hurried into the park to investigate.

"What's going on here?" he demanded suspiciously. Then he did a double take as he recognized Frank and Joe. "Hey! You two are the Hardy boys, aren't you?"

"That's right, officer," Frank replied. "We're working on a case for our dad. We had a trap set for a suspected thief, but then another fugitive showed up and spoiled everything."

Grinning, he pointed at the monkey, who was now nestling contentedly in Biff's arms, scratching itself and staring at the circle of faces watching it.

"Well, I'll be a monkey's uncle!" said the policeman. "You mean that's the one that escaped from the pet shop?"

"Must be," said Joe. "The last time it was seen, I believe it was heading down Ardmore Avenue, which leads right into the park."

"People's heads must be its favorite mode of transportation," Frank added with a chuckle. "That's how it was proceeding on Ardmore Avenue when last observed."

"Next time it tries hopping up and down on my noggin," Chet steamed, "I'm going to tie a knot in the little creep's tail!"

"Relax, and knock on wood, pal," said Joe, patting Chet on the head. "That's probably what confused the poor critter. It thought that round thing on top of your shoulders was part of the tree!"

Joe's wisecrack brought a general round of laughter. Even Chet joined in, with his usual good nature.

The policeman used his walkie-talkie to report the monkey's capture to the station house. The sergeant on duty promised to dispatch a squad car to pick up the escaped animal, so the officer took the monkey and headed back to the park entrance to await its arrival.

Yvor Killian had remained silent in the policeman's presence, which might have been one of the reasons the officer had not recognized him.

"Sorry our trap didn't work," Frank apologized as the boys accompanied the dancer to his car.

Warlord grinned wryly. "Doesn't matter. To tell the truth, I'm a bit relieved. If we had caught the crooks, it might've made the headlines, but I'm not sure how I'd have ended up looking in the eyes of the public. A lot of people might figure I was crooked myself. Plus, I'd be worrying about the thief's pals trying to get even with me for setting him up."

"We'll nail him eventually," Joe promised.

"I don't doubt it." Warlord offered the Hardys and their friends a handshake and added, "Are you coming to see my show?"

"Joe and I'd like to catch the matinee tomorrow," Frank said. "If we can get in."

"No problem. There'll be tickets waiting at the gate for you and your dates."

Frank and Joe looked forward to the performance enthusiastically. Joe invited Iola Morton, and Frank brought Callie Shaw. Arrangements had been made to stage the show in the auditorium in case of rain, but sunshine prevailed so the outdoor performance was to go on as planned.

Since Bayshore College had no football stadium, chairs and a stage had been set up in the grassy quadrangle at the center of the campus.

The show began with two numbers by the college symphony. Then Warlord and his troupe bounded on stage, amid excited shouts and handclapping.

"Ooh, what gorgeous costumes!" gasped Iola.

Warlord was garbed somewhat in the style of a Japanese samurai knight, though in much more brilliant colors. His face was whitened with powder and streaked with war paint, and he was literally armed to the teeth with a variety of knives and a long-bladed sword. The other dancers looked equally stunning and barbaric.

From the first note of their opening number, they held the audience spellbound. The whole troupe formed a pulsing spectacle in color, but Warlord especially riveted all eyes with his breathtaking leaps and twirls as he brandished his blades in gleaming arcs.

"It looks so dangerous!" Callie murmured.

"You're right," said Frank. "But what a showman he is!"

Suddenly Joe became aware of a noisy hum that seemed to clash with the music. As it grew louder, he glanced questioningly at his brother. "Hey, what's that?"

"Sounds like motorcycles!"

The words were hardly out of Frank's mouth when, with an earsplitting din of exhaust, a column of motorcyclists appeared between two buildings and started to charge across the lawn. The riders were masked and leather-jacketed, and bestrode powerful black-and-chrome choppers!

"Are those guys crazy?" Joe blurted, hardly able to believe his eyes.

There were shouts and screams of panic as the audience leaped up and jostled each other in a mad rush to get out of the way. The motorcyclists roared in among them, knocking over chairs and frightening people out of their wits!

Soon the audience and orchestra were scattering in all directions as the masked riders circled around and around the quadrangle. Several of them even roared up the side ramps and across the stage, forcing Warlord and his troupe to take cover.

"Those nuts should be locked up!" Frank shouted. "Come on, Joe. Give me a hand!"

"What can we do?"

Instead of straining his voice to be heard above the engine roar, Frank merely pointed to a coiled firehose on a nearby building. Joe's face lit up.

The Hardys swiftly broke out the wide canvas hose from its wall brackets. Then, while Frank gripped the nozzle and braced himself, Joe spun the valve wheel. A powerful gusher of water shot across the quadrangle as the valve was opened.

"Hang on!" Joe shouted and grabbed the hose before it got away from Frank.

The rogue motorcyclists were enraged by the Hardys' tactic. Some tried to run down the two boys, but the blasting force of the water at pointblank range almost knocked them out of the saddle and forced them to veer away!

Frank and Joe played the hose back and forth, dousing the riders thoroughly. One by one, they scooted out of the quadrangle, rather than get soaked further. The approaching whine of police sirens sped them on their way.

Several police cars soon converged on the campus. The Hardys learned later that an alarm had been telephoned in by a college official who had witnessed the scene from a window overlooking the quadrangle. Unfortunately, the masked riders had fled at top speed before roadblocks could be set up, and there seemed little hope of collaring and identifying any of them.

"Good work, you two!" Sergeant Burton congratulated the Hardy boys. "Did you get a look at any of their faces?"

"No chance, with those masks they were wearing," Frank replied. "But they could have been the Gung-Ho gang."

"I'd bet on it!" said Joe.

"So would I," the burly police sergeant agreed. "Those punks are the worst bunch of motorcycle hoods around here. But there's not much hope of proving it unless the highway patrol manages to nail one of them."

Warlord and his troupe were willing to resume the show. But half the audience had dispersed, and the orchestra was in disarray due to scattered sheet music and several damaged instruments, so it was announced that the performance would be rescheduled at a later date.

"Sorry the show was ruined," Frank said when they took Callie home.

"It certainly wasn't your fault," the pretty blond girl told him with a cheerful smile. "I think it was wonderful the way you and Joe drove off that vicious gang!" Iola agreed.

After a stop at the Mortons' farm, the Hardys drove back to Elm Street. On the way, Joe remarked thoughtfully to his brother, "Think there was any special reason for that motorcycle attack?"

"Good question," Frank responded. "I've been wondering the same thing myself. Breaking up the show that way was really asking for trouble with the police. Seems to me even the Gung-Ho gang wouldn't go that far just for kicks. They must've had a definite motive."

"That's how it looks to me, too. And here's another question," Joe went on. "Did you get the impression any of those punks were gunning for us in particular?"

"Matter of fact I did," Frank said. "When they first showed up, I thought for a while the leader was deliberately steering our way. But there was so much confusion and milling around, he got sidetracked."

Joe flashed his brother a quizzical glance. "So what does it all add up to?"

"If you're asking for a hunch, I'd say it could be more than a coincidence that this should happen right after last night's stakeout. . . . Check?"

"Check! In other words, Warlord helps set up a trap for whoever stole the samurai sword, so the next day his show gets wrecked for revenge!"

"And if you and I were seen last night," Frank added, "that would be enough reason for including *us* in the revenge."

"Right. Assuming our hunch about the identity of the masked riders is correct, it would also mean the Gung-Ho gang must be in cahoots with the gallery thief, who—"

111

As the Hardys turned up Elm Street and could see their home, Joe broke off with a slight exclamation. A familiar blue sedan was parked in front of their house. "Hey! That's Sam Radley's car. I wonder what's up?"

The boys hurried inside and found the operative chatting with their mother. Aside from a much smaller bandage than they had seen him wearing at the hospital, he seemed none the worse for wear.

"No concussion?" Frank queried as they shook hands warmly.

"Nope." Radley grinned. "I woke up this morning raring to go, so they had to turn me loose."

Mrs. Hardy excused herself to attend to some chores, and Sam Radley hastily briefed the two boys on the reason for his visit. He told them that ever since his release from the hospital that morning, he had been keeping watch on the waterfront cafe where he had seen the Japanese gangster meet the American.

"Did you spot the *Yakuza* again?" Joe asked eagerly.

"No, but I did spot the guy he met yesterday." Sam related that his attempt to shadow the man had failed when his quarry leaped aboard a passing bus. "But this time I got a really good look at his face—and I was surer than ever that I'd seen him somewhere before! I drove straight home and checked my files, and sure enough I got a make!"

"Then his photo would probably be in Dad's files, too," Frank put in.

"Of course. I'll show it to you."

112

Fenton Hardy's study was lined with file cabinets bulging with dossiers on every known criminal who had come under his scrutiny. Besides data from his own cases, information had been gleaned from police and FBI sources as well as newspaper accounts.

Sam Radley quickly pulled out a picture from the K drawer and handed it to the Hardy boys. "There's the bird I'm talking about. He's an expert burglar and second-story man named Krunkel."

The photo showed a squint-eyed, hatchet-faced man about forty years old with a receding hairline. As they studied the picture, both boys gasped.

"Hey! That's the guy we saw right after the motor-cycle race!" Joe blurted.

"Right," Frank concurred. "He's the man Len Boggs was talking to!"

14

A Siren Shrieks!

Radley was keenly interested to learn that the Hardys had already come across Krunkel in their investigation of the Satoya case. He was also startled when he heard about the anonymous phone call offering to sell Warlord the stolen samurai sword, and the outcome of last night's stakeout.

"Tough break," the private detective commented. "But at least we've got a definite lead now. I'd say this makes it pretty certain that Krunkel must figure in the case."

Frank and Joe also felt that it confirmed their hunch that the Gung-Ho gang might be in cahoots with the criminals behind the theft of the samurai sword.

"Incidentally, I've got an idea how that gallery heist might have been pulled," Frank added.

"Let's hear it," said Radley.

"The thief couldn't have dropped a line from the roof of the Palmer-Glade Galleries because there are some kind of detectors or sensors up there that would've triggered the alarm. But suppose there are *two* thieves—and they went up separately on the roofs of the buildings on each side of Palmer-Glade."

"Then what?"

"They heave or shoot a line from one to the other, so that it passes over the gallery building without actually touching the roof. They make it fast at both ends and let the middle of the line droop down in front of the Palmer-Glade building's facade."

"I get it!" Joe exclaimed, snapping his fingers. "And then they simply go down the line, hand over hand, to the third-story window where they want to break in."

"Right, or they could use a pulley with a handgrip and slide down. That would give the first man something to hang onto while he cut the pane."

"Pretty smart," said Radley. "I think you've hit on the answer, Frank. What's more, it ties in with Krunkel's usual M.O."

The boys knew that among detectives M.O. stood for *modus operandi,* or a crook's known working methods.

"He generally works with a partner," Radley explained, "and he always comes up with some cute trick to avoid setting off the alarm."

"Does Krunkel operate in the Bayport area?" Joe inquired.

"Not that I know of. Most of his robberies have been around New York or Boston, although he pulled one job in Miami. But now that I've seen him in Shoreham two days in a row, it looks as if he's staying here. I'll check the hotels and motels in this area."

"Good idea," said Frank.

Soon after Radley left, the telephone rang. Joe answered. His face tensed and he beckoned his brother to listen in as a whispering voice came over the line.

"You interested in that Jap sword that got heisted in New York?"

"You could say that," Joe replied. "Who's calling, please?"

"Never mind who I am. And don't bother trying to trace this call. I won't be on the line long enough." The whisperer paused for effect before adding, "I just thought you might like a tip."

"Go ahead. I'm listening."

"Ever hear of Dobert Humber?"

"Sure. He collects rare weapons."

"That's the guy. And he may soon be adding that stolen sword to his collection."

"How come?" Joe asked, exchanging a startled glance with Frank.

"Because he just made a secret deal to buy it from the thief who swiped it!"

There was a click at the other end of the line as the

116

unknown caller hung up. Joe whistled softly and put down the phone. "What do you make of that, Frank?"

"Looks like the thief couldn't make a sale to Warlord last night, so he's trying another customer."

"Right. But how do we find out if the tip's on the level?"

"There's one simple way," said Frank. "Let's get hold of Humber and ask him while we watch his face."

Frank called the collector and requested an appointment. Humber was willing to see the Hardys immediately, so they drove to his house. He invited them into his sitting room.

"Mr. Humber," Frank began, "would you have been interested in bidding on that samurai sword that was stolen from the Palmer-Glade Galleries?"

"Oh, definitely. In fact, I intended to do so. It would make a splendid addition to my collection. Why do you ask?"

"Because we got a tip that you've arranged to buy it from the thief."

Humber's reaction to Frank's bombshell was plain to see. Surprise was written all over his face, but neither boy could see any sign of guilt.

"Why, that's the most ridiculous thing I ever heard!" Humber exclaimed. "How on earth would I be able to get in touch with the thief, when I don't even know who stole the sword? Or is he supposed to have contacted me? Just who told you this fantastic tale, anyhow?"

"An anonymous phone caller."

"No wonder! He wouldn't dare make such an idiotic charge in public, where I could have the law on him! I'd like to get my hands on that lying sneak! I'd soon teach him not to go smearing my good name!" Their freckled host was becoming red-faced with anger as he responded to the charge.

Frank held up his hand with an apologetic smile. "Okay, you don't have to convince us, Mr. Humber. We received the call, so we got in touch with you right away to give you a chance to refute his story. Apparently whoever contacted us either has a screw loose, or has it in for you."

"Any idea who it might be?" Joe asked.

Before Humber could answer, the phone rang. He scooped up the handset impatiently, but a few seconds later the Hardys saw his expression change dramatically.

He beckoned frantically to the boys. Frank and Joe sprang up from their chairs and bent close to listen as he held the receiver slightly away from his ear.

"You can have the sword for ten thousand in cash!" a man on the other end said.

Humber flashed a glance at Frank, who nodded.

"And to whom would I—er, pay this money?" he said into the phone.

"To me."

"How?"

"Ever heard of Lookout Rock?"

"Hm, yes. On the outskirts of Bayport, I believe. In any case, I'm sure I can find it."

"Do that. And be there tonight, at twelve sharp, with the money in a flight bag. Got that?"

"I think so. Midnight at Lookout Rock, and bring the ten thousand dollars in a flight bag," Humber repeated.

"In unmarked bills!" the voice added sharply. "Now listen carefully. Wear a watch, and make sure it's adjusted to the telephone time signal. Lookout Rock's on top of a hill, but when you first arrive, just go halfway up the hillside and wait there. Then, at twelve, start walking toward the rock."

"I understand."

"Good. That's where the exchange will take place. The money for the sword, assuming you're not dumb enough to try doublecrossing me. Any tricks and you'll regret it!"

The receiver was slammed down as the caller rang off. Dobert Humber hung up with a somewhat stunned expression.

"It appears your anonymous tipster wasn't so far wrong after all!" he murmured to the Hardys.

Frank nodded thoughtfully. "He evidently assumed you'd already received the call and accepted."

"If he knew the call was going to be made, he must be one of the thieves himself, or at least in with them somehow," said Joe. "Which sounds like *he's* pulling some kind of doublecross—squealing on his own pals."

"B-B-But should I have agreed?" Humber asked a trifle nervously.

"Sure! It'll give us a chance to trap the thieves and recover the sword!" said Joe.

Frank frowned and tugged his lower lip. "They may be having your house watched, Mr. Humber, to make sure you don't go to the police. They may even have your phone bugged or your line tapped. Would you mind if Joe and I stay here till you leave?"

"Of course not, do by all means! But if the thieves are watching my house and see you Hardys drive away right after me, isn't that likely to put them on guard?"

"It would if they saw us, but I intend to make sure they don't. Your car's in the garage, isn't it?"

"Yes, of course, but—"

"And the garage is attached to the house, so Joe and I could go there without being seen."

Humber's eyes lit up with enthusiasm as he caught on. "You mean you and your brother can be hidden in my car when I drive away!"

"Right, sir."

"Splendid idea, my boy! By jove, how clever. I wish I'd thought of that!"

At quarter after eleven that night, Humber's expensive limousine was driven out of the garage and away from the estate. Humber was at the wheel, the only visible person in the car. A flight bag filled with newspaper sat on the passenger seat next to him. Frank and Joe were huddled on the floor of the back seat compartment.

Meanwhile, two boyish figures could be seen in silhouette through one lighted window of the wealthy collector's mansion. They appeared to be watching the late TV news. Actually they were dummies which Humber had helped the boys rig with great glee. They consisted of stuffed suits of clothes with marble statuary busts fitted in place to serve as heads.

The hill on which Lookout Rock was situated had been the site of the middle cloverleaf in the motorcycle race. A narrow dirt lane ran along the foot of the slope.

Humber parked in a secluded spot and got out without saying a word. Frank and Joe crawled out the other side, which was concealed from view by the surrounding shrubbery. Earlier they had disconnected the courtesy light switch, so that no glow would be visible to give them away when the back door was opened.

Humber started up the hillside first and settled himself to wait at a convenient spot about halfway up the slope. The Hardy boys followed cautiously, keeping low and squirming through the underbrush. Rather than risk going too high and giving themselves away, they picked a hiding place which would afford them an equally clear view of Humber and the massive rocky outcrop on the brow of the hill.

"Got the time?" Joe whispered after a lengthy wait.

"About one minute to twelve," Frank responded softly. "It won't be long now!"

Seconds crept by.

"Now!" Frank hissed as the illuminated dial of his watch showed twelve o'clock.

The Hardys saw Humber rise to his feet, clutching

the flight bag, and start slowly up the slope. Both boys braced themselves to make a sprint toward the rock and try to seize the thief once the exchange was underway.

Suddenly a siren shrieked somewhere below them! Frank and Joe glimpsed Humber's startled reaction, but their eyes were mainly fixed on Lookout Rock.

In the moonlit darkness they saw a figure bolt from cover and dart toward a motorcycle. Its engine roared to life and the rider sped off!

The Hardys raced up the hillside. It was too late to catch the thief, but Frank whipped out a flashlight, playing its beam on the ground. Then he stopped short. "Joe! Take a look at this!" he cried.

15

Police Tip

Joe gasped as he saw the object revealed by the flashlight beam—a sheathed, long-bladed sword lying near the base of Lookout Rock! Its scabbard was of plain, leather-covered metal, but its hilt was beautifully inlaid with mother-of-pearl!

"Just like the photo they showed us at the gallery!" Joe exclaimed, kneeling down for a closer look. "This must be it, all right!"

"Watch out for prints!" Frank warned.

"Don't worry, I'm not going to handle it," Joe replied. "Got some twine here that should do for a carrying handle."

He fished in his pocket and brought out some stout string salvaged from a package, then tied one end to the

123

hilt and the other to the sheath. By gripping the string, the sword could now be picked up without danger of smudging any possible fingerprints.

"Hey! What happened to Humber?" Frank blurted.

His brother glanced down the slope but could see no one. "The car's gone, too!" Joe noted. "He must have taken off the same time as the guy on the motorcycle—that's why we didn't hear him go!"

Frank chuckled dryly. "That siren must've scared him out of his wits. He was probably afraid the police might nab him for buying stolen goods!"

"Speaking of the police—where are they?" Joe wondered aloud.

The boys hurried down the hillside to obtain a better view, unobstructed by trees. After surveying the moonlit lane in both directions, they could see no car of any kind, either police or civilian.

Joe frowned and scratched his head. "Boy, that's funny. Maybe the siren noise we heard was just a police car going by on the main highway."

"Sounded closer than that," Frank said doubtfully.

"Next question. What do we do for transportation? Looks like we're stuck out here with no car."

After a hasty conference, the Hardys decided that one of them would go back to Humber's house to retrieve their car, while the other kept watch on the ransom site, in case the thief or thieves returned to look for their abandoned loot. The boys flipped a coin, and Joe got the job of staying.

"Don't take any chance of being seen," Frank warned his brother. "Pick a spot where you'll be out of sight, and stay there till I get back!"

"Will do," Joe promised.

His wait was shorter than expected. In less than an hour, their yellow car appeared on the dirt lane that bordered the foot of the hillside. Joe scrambled down from his hiding place to join his brother, bringing the samurai sword with him.

"You made good time," he commented, climbing into the car.

"Yes, I had a lucky break," Frank said as he maneuvered to turn the car around. "Phil Cohen tooled along shortly after I made it out to the highway. He was on his way home from a date and gave me a lift to Humber's house."

"Was Humber there?" Joe queried.

"Probably. But the garage was closed and the place was dark, as if everyone had turned in." Frank grinned. "Guess he was trying to give himself an alibi in case the law did come around."

"That guy's a real nitwit," Joe declared. "I wonder what he thought *we'd* say if that police car had picked us up?"

"No telling. He didn't stick around to find out! I guess Warlord had him sized up right," Frank reflected. "Humber's only interest is looking out for Number One. The rest of the human race isn't all that important."

Joe was silent for a minute or two as they drove through the residential suburbs on their way to the downtown area of Bayport. Finally he said, "Now that we've got the sword, do you think it had anything to do with Satoya's disappearance?"

"My hunch is yes," the older Hardy boy mused thoughtfully. "But I can't prove it. Before we'll know the answer to that, we've got to find out whether he disappeared on his own accord or was kidnapped."

"Right! I was thinking about that while I was waiting for you," Joe said. "I've got an idea how Satoya could have pulled his vanishing act."

"Let's hear it."

"It's so simple," Joe explained. "Say the chauffeur is as loyal to his boss as Oyama claims. When he turned into the underground parking garage, he could have stopped the limousine halfway down the ramp, just long enough to let Satoya pop out of the secret compartment. Then he could have continued on and pretended he knew nothing when Oyama searched the car. Meanwhile, all Satoya had to do was turn up his coat collar and slip away through the crowd. At that time, there was a mob of people around the hotel. None of them knew what was going on."

Frank was impressed by his brother's theory. "When you put it that way, it sure sounds obvious, Joe! That's so simple, it's *got* to be the right answer!"

"But where's Satoya hiding?"

"If your deductions are right, he must have arranged

for a place before he ever flew over here. Perhaps a house in an out-of-the-way spot!"

"That figures, with no nosy neighbors to wonder who he is. He could have had somebody rent it for him under a phony name before he arrived."

Frank nodded, keeping a watchful eye out for late-hour traffic as they slowed and crossed an intersection with a blinking yellow light. He looked as though he were already turning over another idea in his mind.

"Joe, suppose Satoya knew beforehand that something was going to happen to the sword—"

"You mean, that someone might try to steal it?"

"Could be. Anyhow, say he went into hiding so he could try to get hold of it himself without anyone knowing what he was up to."

"I'd buy that," said Joe, "especially if the sword had belonged to the Satoya family. Remember what Mr. Shimada told us about how much the samurai class prizes their swords."

"Right! But now that we're turning the sword over to the police, the whole thing's out of his hands. I mean, now there's no possible way Satoya can latch onto it secretly, and nobody else can, either."

The younger Hardy boy shot his brother a keen glance. "What are you getting at, Frank?"

"Just this. If our reasoning is correct, Satoya will no longer have any motive for staying undercover."

"You're right!" Joe snapped his fingers. "Once he

hears the news on television, or reads it in the papers, maybe Satoya will turn up again!"

"Suppose the police decide not to release the news for a while, in order to keep the thieves in the dark."

"Hm. Then how would he find out?"

"We could tip him off."

Joe looked startled. "Are you kidding? How could we do that?"

"Look," Frank replied. "If Satoya disappeared on his own accord, the chauffeur must have helped him. Right?"

"Sure, but how does th—" Joe broke off suddenly as he caught on. "Oh, oh! I get it. If our theory is correct, the chauffeur probably knows where his boss is hiding, so if we tip *him* off, he'll pass the word on to Satoya!"

"Check. But we'd have to do it very casually and naturally. Otherwise the chauffeur might get the notion that we're just trying to trap his master."

"Any ideas?"

"We'll use the sword itself," said Frank. "I just hope we can find him this late at night."

Joe pointed out that every time they had gone to the Bayport Chilton, the chauffeur had been seated in the hotel lobby. "Come to think of it," the younger Hardy boy mused, "maybe Satoya posted him there to report what goes on."

"You could be right," Frank agreed. "If you are, we've got a good chance of finding him there now."

When the boys entered the lobby after parking outside the hotel, the granite-faced chauffeur was sitting in his usual spot. The Hardys hurried toward him. Frank noticed his eyes widen in surprise when he saw the samurai sword that Joe was carrying by the twine handle.

"Do you speak English?" Frank asked.

The chauffeur nodded. "A little."

"Do you know if Mr. Kawanishi or Mr. Oyama is still awake?"

The reply was a shrug. "I do not know. Maybe so."

"Well, look," Frank went on smoothly, "we just recovered this sword that belonged to Mr. Satoya, the one that was stolen in New York. We're taking it to police headquarters, but we thought his company officials might want to know. Only it's late and we're in a hurry, so could you please give them the news?"

The chauffeur looked eager for more information, but seemed at a loss for words. Perhaps, the boys thought, it was because he did not speak English very well.

Instead, the man merely rose from his chair and bowed to the young detectives. "Thank you. I will tell them."

The Hardys strode toward the door.

"Pretty neat, the way you handled that, Frank!" Joe murmured out of the corner of his mouth. "I'll bet he gets on the phone to Satoya as soon as we're out of the lobby!"

As the boys emerged from the hotel, they turned and

129

headed toward their parked car. The downtown area of Bayport looked almost deserted at this late hour. A policeman who was coming along the street eyed them with interest.

Suddenly the young officer's face took on an expression of excitement. He quickened his pace so as to intercept the Hardys before they reached their car.

"Hold it, you two!"

Frank and Joe halted in surprise.

"What's wrong?" Frank inquired.

"Hand over that sword!" the policeman snapped.

Joe started to explain. "We're just taking it to police headquarters."

But the officer cut him short. "Don't give me that! Just hand it over! You're both under arrest for possessing stolen goods!"

Frank guessed that the policeman was probably new to the force and had never heard of the Hardy boys or their famous father. Calmly he advised his brother, "Do as he says, Joe. We'll straighten things out at the station."

The policeman summoned a patrol car by radio, and within a few minutes the Hardys found themselves at police headquarters. Here, after exchanging friendly remarks with the surprised desk sergeant, they were ushered into the office of Police Chief Ezra Collig. The sword was already lying on his desk.

"Sorry about this, fellows!" Looking slightly red-faced, Chief Collig rose to shake hands with the boys. "The whole thing's a mix-up!"

130

The chief explained that the police had received an anonymous phone call shortly after midnight. The unknown caller reported spotting two teenage youths in the Bayport area in possession of the valuable Japanese sword that had been stolen from the Palmer-Glade Galleries in New York.

"We put out a radio bulletin telling all officers to be on the lookout," Collig continued, "and I came to the office on purpose to supervise the search, because the tipster knew what he was talking about. But I certainly never expected that you Hardys would be caught in the dragnet!"

"Neither did we," Frank said wryly. "Matter of fact we were on our way here when we got nabbed." He filled the chief in on the night's events and added, "We were hoping the lab might turn up some prints, either on the sword hilt or the sheath."

"Good idea. I'll have them both dusted," the chief promised. "But first, there's someone I want you to meet. He just walked into the station tonight, literally out of the blue sky!"

Collig picked up the phone and gave a brief order. A few moments later, a young Japanese man was escorted into his office. The newcomer, who had glasses and long, dark hair, was well dressed in a gray silk business suit and looked studious but athletic. The police chief introduced him as Toshiro Muramoto.

"Mr. Muramoto has flown over here from Japan, at his own expense, I might add," Collig continued. "I think you fellows ought to hear what he has to say."

Muramoto bowed politely to the Hardys, who

131

returned his gesture. "I understand you two are attempting to solve the disappearance of the man who calls himself Takashi Satoya."

"That's right." Frank frowned. "But why do you say the man who *calls* himself Takashi Satoya?"

"Because that person who landed here in America three nights ago was an impostor!"

16

A Startling Challenger

The Hardys stared in amazement at the Japanese.

"That's a pretty drastic statement," Frank said, "especially if you're asking us to believe that he could fool Satoya's two top senior aides!"

"You raise a good point," Muramoto acknowledged. "One would have to draw one's own conclusions as to whether the two gentlemen were truly deceived."

The young detectives exchanged quick glances.

"Can you prove what you're saying," Joe asked, "about the missing man being an impostor?"

Muramoto nodded firmly. "I can, indeed. What is more, I shall do so, using that sword on the police chief's desk as the main evidence."

He declared he would give the man who called himself Satoya until ten o'clock the next morning to come to police headquarters and answer his accusation. "If he fails to appear," Muramoto added, "I shall then be forced to expose him to the press as a fraud!"

After leaving police headquarters, the Hardys sped back to the Bayport Chilton Hotel to report this startling development to Mr. Kawanishi and Mr. Oyama.

On the way, Joe muttered suspiciously, "Does the timing of all this strike you as a bit fishy, Frank?"

"I'll say it does! If Muramoto needed that samurai sword to prove his accusation, how did he know we'd get it back tonight?"

"Right! That's exactly what I'm wondering. What would he have used as proof without it? Did he just fly over here on the chance that the sword would turn up by the time he landed in Bayport?"

Frank puckered his forehead thoughtfully. "When you come right down to it, it almost sounds like a put-up job, doesn't it?"

"You think Muramoto could have been mixed up in the theft of the sword, and that ransom deal tonight?"

"You've got me, Joe. But I'd like to know the answer. To quote that word you used a minute ago, there must be something fishy somewhere!"

However, when the Hardys reached the hotel and expressed their suspicions to the two senior aides, neither Japanese agreed.

"It is most unlikely that Muramoto would take part in

any criminal plot to have our employer branded as an impostor," Kawanishi pointed out. "To do so would harm his own financial interest."

"How come?" Frank inquired.

The aide explained that the value of a company's stock partly depended on how well the company was managed. If news came out that the Satoya Corporation was run by some fraudulent mystery man posing as the real Takashi Satoya, many investors would lose confidence in the company and would try to sell off whatever shares they owned. This would cause the value of the stock to fall sharply.

"It so happens that young Muramoto owns a large block of stock in the Satoya Corporation," Mr. Kawanishi continued. "So he would suffer a heavy loss. His stock would be worth many millions of yen less than it is worth now, perhaps several hundred thousand dollars in your own money."

"Wow!" Joe whistled softly. "That's a lot of money to lose, just for spilling some bad news!"

Mr. Oyama nodded, confirming what his associate had just told the boys. "You see, young Muramoto's uncle, Akira Muramoto, was an army general in the Second World War. He was also a good friend of our employer. After the war, he became head of a Tokyo bank and lent Mr. Satoya enough money to start his company. In return, he was given a large block of stock in the Satoya Corporation."

The aide added that General Muramoto was now dead, but that his stock had been inherited by his nephew whom the Hardys had just met.

"Naturally," Mr. Oyama concluded, "we find it hard to believe that young Muramoto would cause any scandal that might harm our company. In fact, he would be far more apt to try and cover up any bad news, if he could properly do so."

"It is difficult to guess what has given him this wild idea that our employer is an impostor," said the other aide. "But I think he must sincerely believe it is so."

The Hardys drove home from the hotel thoroughly mystified by this latest surprising twist in the Satoya case. Both were eager to find out what would happen the following day.

Shortly before ten o'clock the next morning, they returned to police headquarters. Toshiro Muramoto was already waiting in Chief Collig's office, and Satoya's two senior aides, Mr. Kawanishi and Mr. Oyama, arrived soon afterward.

Presently Muramoto glanced at his wristwatch. "It is now almost one minute past ten o'clock," he announced. "The deadline has expired."

Chief Collig looked at the two company aides, who merely shrugged. Then his gaze turned back to Muramoto. "We're all waiting to hear what you have to say, sir."

"Very well. I had hoped to give the man who calls himself Takashi Satoya a chance to defend himself.

136

Since he is not here, I can only assume that he is afraid to face me. This confirms my suspicion that he is an impostor."

"You still haven't told us why you suspect him in the first place," Frank Hardy put in.

"Is the reason not obvious?" Muramoto shot back. "Here is a man who heads one of the world's greatest corporations—yet he is afraid to be seen in public. For years now he has avoided reporters and cameras and hidden himself away from the outside world. Why else would he be so secretive, except that he fears being exposed as a fake!"

Joe spoke up. "Then what do you think happened to the *real* Mr. Satoya?"

Muramoto's eyes flashed at the two company aides, and he pointed his finger at them accusingly. "I think those two can answer your question better than I can."

"Why, sir?"

"Because I believe they have done away with the real Takashi Satoya! They were his closest associates, so they are the only ones who could have pulled such a crime and still escaped detection. In his place, they have substituted an impostor who is completely under their control. Through him, they have been able to run the company for their own profit!"

There was a moment of startled silence as Muramoto finished speaking.

Then Frank said, "If you're right, why has this so-called impostor disappeared?"

"Probably because they knew he would soon be exposed as a fake. So long as they keep him out of sight and pretend he has 'disappeared,' no one can prove they've committed any crime."

All eyes swung toward the two aides. Both looked perfectly calm.

The tall, burly Mr. Kawanishi spoke first. "You ask why our revered employer became a hermit who prefers to keep out of the public eye. The reason is no mystery. Ten years ago, his wife and children were killed in an air crash."

"Their deaths were a terrible blow," said Mr. Oyama. "For a time he felt he had nothing more to live for. Ever since then he has shunned the outside world and lives mostly at his villa, where he devotes himself to gardening and studying the way of life called Zen."

"It is true that he runs the company by issuing orders through us," Kawanishi went on. "But that is his own wish, because it enables him to keep his privacy. However, he telephoned us last night, and we are happy to announce that he will reappear in Bayport this morning, to answer your charges in person."

Mr. Kawanishi, who was seated near the office windows, had been glancing out at the street below, and now he spoke with a slight smile. "In fact, I believe our revered employer has just arrived."

There was a stir of excitement. Moments later the telephone rang on Chief Collig's desk. Soon after he answered, an erect, gray-haired man with a wispy mustache was ushered into the office—the same man Frank and Joe had seen alight from the Satoya jet plane in the Bayport airfield!

Toshiro Muramoto stared keenly at the elderly newcomer, who responded with a polite bow.

"I understand you accuse me of being an impostor," he said to Muramoto.

"I do, indeed! And I shall now *prove* my accusation!"

"Pray do so, by all means."

It was Muramoto's turn to bow. "Very well. I shall do so by means of a test—using that beautiful samurai sword, which has belonged to the Satoya family for over four hundred years."

As Muramoto moved to pick up the sword from the police chief's desk, Frank asked if the sword had been dusted for prints. Chief Collig reported that this had been done, but that no fingerprints had been found, indicating that sheath, hilt and blade had all been carefully wiped clean.

Muramoto then proceeded with his demonstration. "It is well known to many close friends and business associates of the *real* Takashi Satoya," he went on, "that this sword has a secret compartment concealed in its hilt. It was designed centuries ago by the expert swordsmith who forged the blade."

The gray-haired tycoon nodded. "That is so. The secret knowledge of how to open it was passed down only to male members of the family."

His two aides murmured their agreement.

139

"Good!" said the bespectacled Muramoto. "If there is no argument on that score, it will give you a way to prove that you are, indeed, the real Takashi Satoya. I suggest you show us that you can open the secret compartment."

He held out the sword.

"Of course! I am happy to accept your challenge," said the tycoon, taking the weapon.

His face was calm as he began to finger certain points on the hilt. But his expression slowly changed—at first to a frown of surprise, then to bewilderment, and finally to outright dismay.

"Something is wrong!" he exclaimed.

"So it appears," said Muramoto sarcastically.

Satoya's two aides appeared dumbfounded.

Their employer made one or two final desperate attempts to open the secret compartment before giving up. "This cannot be the real sword!" he declared. "Someone has substituted a forgery!"

"Indeed?" Muramoto sneered. "How strange that you did not notice the switch until it turned out that you were unable to discover the mechanism of the secret compartment!"

Glancing at the Hardy boys and Police Chief Collig, he added, "I believe these impartial witnesses will now agree that I have proved my accusation beyond any doubt."

All three stared at the man who called himself Satoya. His only response was a helpless, tight-lipped shrug.

"In that case," Muramoto continued, "I shall now issue an announcement to the press, telling how I have proved this man to be an impostor. I shall then cable the Japanese government in Tokyo, officially requesting that they take over control of the Satoya Corporation, until the police can find out what happened to the real Satoya."

Kawanishi and Oyama both sprang to their feet, with looks of consternation on their faces.

"Wait! If you do that, it will play havoc with the operation of the company!" one cried.

"Not only that—the value of our company stock will plunge disastrously on the stock exchange! People who have invested heavily in shares of the Satoya Corporation will lose millions of yen!"

"You are quite right, gentlemen," Muramoto said regretfully. "As a major stockholder, I myself shall be one of the biggest losers. But my honor demands no less. My late uncle, General Akira Muramoto, was a longtime friend of Takashi Satoya's. If you two or anyone else have harmed him or done away with him, my uncle would certainly wish justice to be done and the guilty parties punished, no matter how many millions of yen it might cost."

Suddenly Frank cut in. "Mr. Muramoto, may I make a request?"

The bespectacled young Japanese said, "I promise nothing, but I am certainly willing to listen."

"From what my brother and I have just heard, it may

141

wreck the company if you go ahead and make your accusation public. But I think even you will admit that this whole situation is a mystery."

"The only mystery, I'm afraid, is what has happened to the real Takashi Satoya."

"Put it that way if you like," Frank said. "But at least give Joe and me a chance to solve the mystery. All we ask is twenty-four hours before you take such a drastic step."

Chief Collig added, "What they're asking certainly sounds reasonable to me, sir. I can assure you these young fellows are no mean sleuths. They've been trained by their father—who's probably the greatest criminal investigator in America—and they've solved a number of important cases."

Muramoto hesitated before replying, his forehead creased in a frown. But at last he nodded reluctantly. "Very well. I shall wait until this same time tomorrow morning before calling in the press or cabling my government—but no longer!" Bowing to everyone, he turned on his heel and strode out of the office.

Satoya, or the man who was impersonating him, flashed Frank and Joe a grateful look.

"Young men, I am much indebted to both of you— perhaps even more than you realize," he declared. "If you care to accompany me back to my hotel, I shall explain the reason for my disappearance."

17

Jungle Nightmare

Frank and Joe were eager to hear Satoya's story and readily accepted his invitation. His black limousine was waiting at the curb, with the stony-faced chauffeur at the wheel. The Hardy boys rode in the back seat with the tycoon, while his two senior aides—Kawanishi and Oyama—followed in a separate car.

"My story begins many years ago, in the closing months of World War II," Satoya told them. "Your General MacArthur had begun to recapture the Philippines, and it was only a question of time before the Americans would invade Japan herself."

A certain group of Japanese officers, he related, felt that an honorable surrender was the best course to take, rather than wait for their country to be devastated by bombing and invasion.

One of the group was Takashi Satoya. Although he was only a young lieutenant, he volunteered to carry the group's written, signed surrender offer to the Americans, concealed in the secret compartment of his sword hilt. But on the way he was badly wounded during a strafing attack by American fighter planes, and then taken prisoner.

"For weeks I lay unconscious or delirious in a jungle hospital," the tycoon went on. "By the time I recovered, my sword was gone. Either it was still lying back at the spot where I was wounded, or perhaps it had been picked up by some American GI or Filipino resistance fighter."

"And the surrender offer was lost with it?" Frank inquired.

"Precisely."

"Didn't you tell the Americans who captured you about the surrender document you'd been carrying?" asked Joe.

"I tried to, but no one would believe me. I imagine they thought I was still out of my head with fever, or else that my story was a trick to help me gain special treatment."

Because the surrender offer never reached the proper U.S. authorities, the war wound down to its grim conclusion, including the atom-bombing of Hiroshima and Nagasaki.

"Later, after the war was over," Satoya said, "the

officers who had taken part in the surrender plan met in Tokyo and agreed to keep the whole story secret."

"But why?" said Frank. "By that time I should think most people would have felt you were absolutely right."

"So it may seem to you now, in the United States, but there were still many in Japan who felt otherwise, especially among the samurai class. Some of the older, stiff-necked military men thought we should all have died for the Emperor. They would have called us cowards and traitors had the truth leaked out."

Even today, the Japanese tycoon told the Hardys, some of his countrymen might react the same way.

"For myself, I do not care," Satoya added. "I am an old man. What other people think of me is no longer important. For that matter, most of the senior officers who were involved in the surrender attempt, such as General Muramoto—are now dead. But even so, the truth might cause shame to their families if it became known."

"Then in a way," said Joe, "you're actually protecting the general's nephew, Toshiro Muramoto, who's over here calling you a faker."

Satoya smiled dryly at Joe's remark. "That is so. Life plays strange tricks at times. In any case, the only way I could make sure that the story never came out was to find my lost sword and destroy the surrender document hidden inside the hilt."

"So that's why you were so eager to buy the sword!" Frank commented.

"Exactly. It was also my main reason for coming to the United States, rather than risk entrusting the job to someone else. I intended to make sure that no one outbid me at the auction, and then to destroy the surrender document as soon as the sword was in my hands."

The limousine had now arrived at the Bayport Chilton Hotel. Frank and Joe accompanied Mr. Satoya inside and went up in the elevator to his private suite. He telephoned room service to order tea and resumed his story without inviting Mr. Kawanishi or Mr. Oyama to join them.

"You still haven't told us how or why you disappeared," Frank reminded the gray-haired industrialist.

"I was just coming to that," Satoya replied. "The fact is, I had begun to suspect that there was a traitor in the company—probably a top-rank executive."

The Hardys were startled. The tycoon's words seemed to confirm their father's theory!

"What gave you that idea?" Joe asked.

"Two things. First, someone has recently been leaking information on our business to a competitor, a company called Gorobei Motors. The information included data that was only known to me and my two top aides."

"You mean Mr. Kawanishi and Mr. Oyama?"

Takashi Satoya nodded grimly. "Correct. Also there have been several attempts on my life."

"Wow!" Joe blurted. "You actually think one of them might have tried to kill you?"

"To tell the truth, I do not know what to think. But one thing seemed clear. This trip to the USA would give the guilty party a good chance to have me murdered—and then to blame the crime on American terrorists or assassins. That is why I decided to disappear. It seemed the best way to ensure my own safety. Also, by secretly watching Kawanishi and Oyama, I hoped to discover which one was the traitor."

To accomplish this, Mr. Satoya had arranged to have the hotel rooms of his two senior aides electronically bugged.

"When your limousine arrived at the hotel from the airport," Frank put in, "your other aide, Mr. Ikeda, was unconscious. Did you anesthetize him somehow?"

The gray-haired Japanese nodded. "Yes, I must confess that I did. While he was busy looking out the window on the other side of the car, I suddenly jabbed him with a hypodermic needle, using a quick-acting anesthetic. It started to take effect almost immediately, before he could collect his wits enough to make any outcry. I am ashamed to tell you this, but it seemed the best way to carry out my scheme."

Once Ikeda was unconscious, the tycoon had vanished exactly as the Hardy boys had deduced. He had hidden in the limousine's secret compartment and then had his chauffeur let him out of the car when it was halfway down the ramp, out of sight from both the street and the basement parking garage. The chauffeur, in fact, had been his only confidant, and was the one who had bugged Kawanishi's and Oyama's hotel rooms.

"One more question, sir," said Frank. "Have you any idea at all as to how or why a duplicate sword could have been substituted for your family sword?"

Mr. Satoya shook his head helplessly. "I am relying on you two young men to solve that mystery. I can only assume that it is part of a plot to wrest the company away from my control."

The Hardys promised to do their best to solve the case as soon as possible. Satoya's chauffeur drove them back to police headquarters to pick up their car.

As they headed homeward, Joe switched on the car radio to check the time. An announcer was reading the news. Suddenly he said:

"A flash has just been handed to me. That missing Japanese businessman, Mr. Takashi Satoya, has now turned up again—or at any rate, a person who calls himself Satoya has turned up. He's reported to have walked into Bayport police headquarters just a short time ago. But now he's accused of being an impostor! A major stockholder in the Satoya Corporation has flown here from Japan to make the charge."

The announcer added, "This is the second report to come over the news wires this morning on this strange case. For those of you who missed our earlier story—it was learned this morning that the valuable Japanese samurai sword stolen from the Palmer-Glade Auction Galleries in New York was found last night somewhere near Bayport. According to one unconfirmed report, this sword belonged to the real Takashi Satoya. We will keep you posted on any further developments in the story as they come in."

"Sufferin' catfish!" Joe exclaimed. "I wonder if Muramoto broke his promise about giving us twenty-four hours to crack the case?"

"Sure sounds that way," Frank gritted. "This means we've really got to work fast!"

When they arrived home on Elm Street, Aunt Gertrude was waiting eagerly to quiz them about what had happened at police headquarters. Before the boys could satisfy her curiosity, the telephone rang. Frank answered. The caller was Sam Radley.

"What's up, Sam?" Frank inquired.

"I've finally run down Krunkel and his partner!"

"You mean you've got them under arrest?"

"Not yet. I figured it might be better to keep them under observation for a while and see what we can learn from them."

"Smart idea!" Frank agreed.

Radley explained that he had shown Krunkel's photo to the desk clerks of various hotels and motels in the Shoreham area, and had finally located the place where the squint-eyed burglar was staying. He and another man named Darbold, who was a known accomplice of Krunkel's, had registered at the Seneca Motel on Main Street.

"I've got the place staked out," Sam added, "but

there'll be two suspects to watch—so I may need help. Could you and Joe lend me a hand?"

"You bet!" said Frank. "Tell us where to meet you, and we'll be there in a jiffy!"

A short time later the two youths walked into a coffee shop across the street from the Seneca Motel. Radley was seated in a booth by the front window, nursing a cup of coffee.

"Great work, Sam!" Frank congratulated the operative as the Hardys joined him.

"Have either of them shown yet?" asked Joe.

"Not yet, but it's past noon, so they ought to be coming out soon to get something to eat. When I showed the desk clerk Krunkel's mug shot, he told me they were still in their room."

"Any chance they could have slipped out when you phoned us?"

"No way. I called you from that booth in the corner, which has a clear view of the motel."

The boys ordered hamburgers and wolfed them down with hearty appetites. They tensed with excitement as Radley suddenly exclaimed, "There's our man!"

A tall figure had just emerged from the motel. Sure enough, it was the hawk-faced man whom the Hardys had seen talking to Len Boggs after the motorcycle race! He made his way toward one of the cars in the motel parking lot.

Radley flipped a coin to see who would follow him. The Hardy boys won.

"Maybe it's just as well," Sam commented. "I think Krunkel might recognize me quicker than he would you two. But be mighty careful, fellows! This guy has no record of violence, but you never can tell."

"We'll watch it, Sam," they promised.

Frank and Joe hurried outside and reached their own car just as Krunkel was pulling away in a sleek, silver-colored, foreign-made coupe.

He headed for the road leading southwest out of Shoreham. It was not a main highway, so the Hardys had to keep a considerable distance behind their suspect to avoid arousing wariness, especially when he turned off on a wooded, dirt road.

As a further precaution, Frank drove past the turn-off, then U-turned a little way farther on. Coming back to the dirt road, he nosed their yellow sporty-looking car slowly along the same route Krunkel had taken. Soon they sighted the silver coupe some distance ahead.

"There it is!" Joe exclaimed.

Apparently Krunkel had pulled off the road and gotten out. Frank maneuvered their own car in among some trees where it would be well concealed from view. Then the boys hastily closed in on Krunkel on foot.

Krunkel's destination turned out to be an old abandoned farmhouse. The house itself was a weather-beaten, ramshackle structure with a sagging roof and boarded-up windows, and the surrounding fields were overgrown with weeds.

Creeping up through the tall grass and underbrush, the Hardys saw Krunkel shining a flashlight down a well.

"What's he looking for?" Joe hissed.

"Search me," Frank whispered back.

Presently the tall, hawk-faced crook straightened up and returned to his car. As soon as they heard him drive away, the two boys rushed toward the well. Frank pulled out a pocket flashlight and aimed it downward.

"Jumpin' Jupiter!" Joe gasped as they saw what the beam revealed.

At the bottom of the well lay a long, sheathed Japanese sword!

18

Gang Wheels

The glimmering light revealed the sword's beautifully decorated hilt.

"It's the *real* sword that Satoya lost during the war!" Frank declared. "It must be!"

"Check," Joe agreed. "There can't be more than two that look that much alike. Wait a minute—!" He broke off suddenly and snapped his fingers. "Frank, I'll bet Krunkel heard the news about that other sword turning up in Bayport—so he came to make sure this one was still here!"

"That makes sense, all right," Frank nodded. "All we have to do now is fish it out of the well."

"Wonder how Krunkel stashed it there and expects to get it up again?"

"Dunno. He's an expert cat burglar. Maybe he's got

some kind of folding ladder in his car. But my guess is one of us will have to go down on a rope."

"You're right," said Joe. "We've got some in the car. Let's go get it."

However, after hiking back to the spot where they had parked, they discovered the red radio signal light was flashing on their dashboard. Joe quickly switched on the transceiver and spoke into the microphone.

"H-2 here. Come in, please."

"This is L calling," said his mother's voice. "You two just had an urgent call from your foreign client at the hotel. He wants to see you as soon as possible."

"Thanks, Mom! Will you phone him back, please, and tell him we're on our way."

"Roger. Ten-four."

Joe hung up the mike and shot a questioning glance at his brother. "She must mean Satoya! Think we should take time to recover the sword first?"

"Better not," Frank voted. "It may be a tricky job and that call sounds urgent. I'm sure the sword will be safe if we leave it here for a while."

"Right! Let's get going!"

The Hardys crowded the speed limit on their way back to Bayport. At the Bayport Chilton Hotel, they phoned Satoya's room from the lobby and were told to come right up.

"I received a startling phone message about half an hour ago," the tycoon informed the boys when they arrived in his suite.

"From whom, sir?" Frank asked.

"From my junior aide, Haruki Ikeda. He told me he has established contact with the gallery thief, and that he can get my real sword back for one hundred thousand dollars in ransom money!"

The Hardys gaped in astonishment at this unexpected news.

"Did he give you any details?" Joe queried.

Satoya shook his head. "No. From the noises in the background, there seemed to be other people around, and he told me he could not speak freely."

"What did you say?"

"I stalled him off by saying that I needed time to decide whether or not it was wise to deal with a criminal. So he said he would call back in a little while to get my answer."

Frank and Joe exchanged shrewd glances. As often happened because of their close relationship, the two brothers could almost tell what the other was thinking. Frank cocked a quizzical eyebrow, and Joe responded with a slight nod.

"Look, sir!" the older Hardy boy said, turning back to Mr. Satoya. "When Ikeda calls, our advice is to tell him you accept the deal."

It was the tycoon's turn to look astonished. "Are you asking me to trust a thief? What if his offer turns out to be a fraud?"

"As a matter of fact, it probably is," said Frank. "But

if our hunch is right, we may be able to trap the thief, and get back both your sword *and* the money!"

The telephone rang even before Frank finished speaking. Mr. Satoya frowned and plucked nervously at his wispy mustache, then scooped up the handset and answered.

The short conversation that followed was in Japanese. When it was over, the tycoon hung up and turned to face the Hardys again.

"As you have no doubt guessed, that was Ikeda. I have authorized him to draw out the ransom money in cash from the account which our company has opened at the local bank."

Although Satoya did not say so, both boys knew what he was leaving unsaid—namely that he was risking one hundred thousand dollars to back their hunch.

It was not a very comfortable thought.

But Frank replied confidently, "If you'll come with us, sir, Joe and I have something important to show you. When you see it, I think you'll agree the risk is worthwhile."

Satoya's dark eyes were keen and cold, but he inclined his head politely. "Very well, young man. I shall do as you say."

Joe got into the back seat of their yellow car, leaving the Japanese tycoon to sit in front beside Frank. Soon they were on their way out of town.

As they retraced the route they had traveled not long

before, the Hardys explained to Mr. Satoya where they were taking him.

"Joe and I know where the Satoya sword is hidden," Frank began. "So if the offer Ikeda phoned you about is on the level, that means the thief will have to go there to get the sword."

"And that's when we'll nail him!" Joe added zestfully.

Mr. Satoya digested this news with a thoughtful frown. "Do I gather you already know who the thief is?"

Frank nodded as he steered the car along the country road. "Yes, sir, I think we do."

"Yet at the hotel you implied the ransom offer was a fraud."

"I was simply referring to the story Ikeda told you."

"Perhaps you'd better explain that remark, young man."

"Well, sir, the only thing that seems fairly certain," the elder Hardy boy reasoned, "is that whoever planned this whole caper must have known beforehand that you were coming to America, and that you wanted that sword at the Palmer-Glade Galleries."

"I agree," Satoya nodded.

"We can probably count out your jet crew," Frank went on, "and I guess your chauffeur is too faithful to be suspected."

"Yes, that is so."

"Which leaves only your aides as suspects."

"Of course," the tycoon responded impatiently. "I have already told you that the traitor in my company must be either Kawanishi or Oyama."

158

"You're leaving out somebody," Joe reminded him.

"You mean . . .?"

"Ikeda, sir."

Satoya frowned again. "But as I informed you this morning, only my two *senior* aides would have known the data that was leaked to Gorobei Motors."

"But isn't it possible," Frank pointed out, "that someone else in your company may have gotten hold of the same information, either by tapping their phones or rifling their desks and files?"

"Hmm. . . . Now that you put it that way, I suppose such a thing is possible."

"Anyway, there's no use guessing," Frank concluded. "If we're lucky, we may soon know the ans—"

He broke off suddenly, and Joe saw his brother staring keenly into the rear-view mirror.

"What's the matter, Frank?"

"We've got company!"

Almost at that same moment, Joe's ears caught a rising engine sound. Turning his head, he saw a group of motorcyclists behind them.

"Gallopin' guppies! That looks like the Gung-Ho gang!"

"You guessed it," Frank gritted. "And something tells me they've recognized our car!"

The Hardys were skilled auto mechanics and kept their car engine tuned for top performance. Frank made sure everyone's seat belt was fastened, then stepped on the gas. He was too good a driver to take

159

foolish chances, but Fenton Hardy had trained his sons carefully in evasive driving tactics, and the boys knew every street in the Bayport area.

By dodging and circling back and forth through a network of back roads, Frank gradually managed to shake off their pursuers. Joe flashed his brother an approving grin in the rear-view mirror, and even Mr. Satoya murmured, "Well done, young man!"

At last they reached the dirt lane to which they had trailed Krunkel. Frank parked in the same concealed spot they had used before. Then Satoya and the Hardys walked toward the deserted farmhouse. The sword was still in the well.

The group hid but had not long to wait before an approaching car was heard. A compact green station wagon pulled to a halt on the now rutted, weed-choked path that had once been the entrance lane to the farm. A man got out of the car.

It was Haruki Ikeda!

19

The Fearless Three

At the sight of his crew-cut junior aide, Mr. Satoya gave an angry gasp and started to burst out of their hiding place in a clump of shrubbery and underbrush. But Frank restrained him.

"Let's see what he does first," the elder Hardy boy whispered softly.

Opening the station wagon's tailgate, Ikeda took out what seemed to be a ladder of lightweight, flexible metal cable. He carried this up the lane and lowered it into the dried well shaft after hooking it securely to the lip of the well.

As the hidden trio watched, they saw the slim Japanese maneuver cautiously for a footing, and then disappear from view as he climbed down the ladder.

When he reappeared several minutes later, he was clutching the samurai sword! Ikeda wore a smug grin of satisfaction.

This time there was no holding Satoya back. The gray-haired tycoon sprang to his feet, shouting angrily in Japanese. Frank and Joe jumped up and ran after him, seeing that there was no point in continuing to hide.

Ikeda stood motionless for a moment, then his face took on an expression of dumbfounded dismay. But suddenly he seemed to pull himself together and dashed toward his station wagon!

He was still clutching the sword as he reached his car and yanked open the door. Flinging the weapon inside, he slid behind the wheel and tried to gun the engine to life.

In his eagerness to get away, he apparently flooded the engine, and twice it failed to start. Frank and Joe felt afterward that they might have reached the car in time to stop him.

But just then the whine and roar of motorcycle engines caught their attention. The noise was rapidly swelling in volume, and a second later a horde of riders blasted into view between the scattered trees fringing the abandoned farm.

"It's the Gung-Ho gang!" Joe cried, recognizing the mounted hoodlums for the second time that afternoon.

The same thought was going through both boys' minds. *Somehow the gang must have picked up their*

162

trail after Frank thought he had given them the slip, and now the Hardys and their companion were in for trouble!

Obviously the first tactic of Len Boggs and his street punks, Frank realized, would be to try and run them down.

"Come on! Head for the farmhouse!" he cried to Joe and Mr. Satoya.

The trio reached the farmhouse porch only yards ahead of their pursuers. Frank kicked open the door that was hanging by a single hinge, and they plunged inside!

Len Boggs, leading the motorcyclists, tried to chase them right up the porch steps and into the house. But the rotten structure collapsed under the weight of his heavy bike!

There were moments of confusion. Boggs was scarlet with fury as he extricated himself and his motorcycle from the debris.

Realizing that their machines were no longer of any use for purposes of attack, the Gung-Ho's dismounted and began smashing their way into the farmhouse through every possible opening. Most of the gang swarmed in through the windows, after ripping away the boards. Several others gained entry through the long-since stairless back door.

As a seasoned warrior, Mr. Satoya calmly took charge—somewhat to the Hardys' surprise—and suggested that the boys stand back-to-back with him to

163

repel their attackers, though not too close together. Instead of the famous British square, favored by the oldtime redcoats when surrounded and outnumbered, the three formed a human triangle, each several feet away from the others.

Frank and Joe were astonished at the elderly Japanese gentleman's fighting ability. It was clear that he was expertly trained in the martial arts. The boys were too busy swinging their fists or throwing occasional karate kicks to do more than throw him a hasty glance from time to time, in case he required help.

From the looks of things, no such help was likely to be needed. Mr. Satoya coolly whirled and weaved and ducked with the smooth precision of a ballet dancer— and at every move, another attacker seemed to go flying!

Frank and Joe grinned, recognizing his slick evasive technique as that of aikido, by which the attacker's own momentum is turned back against himself.

The Hardys relied more on old-fashioned American punches to discourage their opponents, and these seemed to work equally well.

One by one, the panting Gung-Ho's seemed to lose heart and fall back to let others do the fighting. At last they were actually watching, more like spectators than participants.

Moments later, as Frank uncorked a hard right that sent an attacker spinning back against the wall, one gang member exclaimed admiringly, "Hey, man! These dudes are *good!*"

When Joe also decked an opponent with his fist, and Mr. Satoya sent another man flying over his shoulder, the gang suddenly burst out laughing and applauding.

The Hardys could scarcely believe their eyes and ears. They and their elderly companion had fought the Gung-Ho's to a standstill, and now they were getting cheers instead of blows. Like Horatius defending the bridge of Rome with his two friends, by their spunky fight they had actually won over their enemies!

"If you can't lick 'em, join 'em!" one motorcyclist chuckled and stuck out his hand toward Frank. "Put 'er there, pal!"

Frank hesitated a moment, suspecting a trick, but then grinned and responded to the offered handshake. "Suits me."

Other gang members crowded around to join in the handshaking and smoke the figurative peace pipe.

"Hey, Pop!" one said to Satoya. "Where'd you learn all those trick judo throws?"

"Aikido, actually," the Japanese tycoon corrected. "I learned it in a martial arts *dojo* in my native land, many years before you were born, young man. If you too wish to learn the art, perhaps that can be arranged. My company may soon open a plant here in the Bayport area. When this happens, I shall give orders for an instructor to be sent over as part of the staff. He will teach you young men to be true samurai—not dangerous jackals or bullies."

The Gung-Ho's took his reproof with good-natured

respect and heartily applauded the announcement. Mr. Satoya was clearly pleased. He seemed more at ease with these high-spirited, roughneck gang members than he had in the polite surroundings of the Bayport Chilton Hotel.

"What did you guys jump us for, anyhow?" Joe asked.

The motorcyclists grinned sheepishly and shrugged.

"No special reason," one said. "We were just tooling along when we spotted your car. Len Boggs talked us into chasing you. I think he's still sore 'cause your brother beat him in the Hare Scrambles race."

The gang leader reddened at this, but finally and reluctantly came forward to shake hands with the Hardys.

"What're you guys doin' out here?" another motor-cyclist asked. "Solvin' another mystery?"

"Trying to," Frank replied. "We almost had a crook collared before you Gung-Ho's showed up. Now he's taken off."

Suddenly an idea occurred to Frank. "Hey, how would you like to give us a hand?" he said.

"Why not?" a gang member replied. "What's the deal?"

"Did you notice that green station wagon that was parked near the road when you first got here?"

"Sure, what about it?"

"Have you guys got CB radios on your bikes?"

"Most of us have. Why?"

"How would you like to fan out from here," Frank proposed, "and see if you can spot where that wagon went?"

"I will pay a one-hundred-dollar reward to the first man who sights it," Mr. Satoya promised.

The Gung-Ho's exploded with enthusiasm. They all hurried out to their motorcycles. Soon the gang was roaring off in all directions in pursuit of the fugitive.

Frank and Joe returned to their car with Mr. Satoya. Frank tuned in their radio to the proper frequency, and the three waited tensely for news.

At last a voice crackled over their speaker. "Len Boggs calling the Hardys!"

"Hardys here. We read you," Frank replied. "Come in, please! Any luck, Len?"

"You bet! I've spotted your green station wagon!"

20

Black Commandos

The Hardys felt a thrill of excitement at Len Boggs's report. Both sensed that the case was nearing a climax, and that luck was giving them another chance to trap the traitor inside the Satoya Corporation, the culprit behind the mystery of the samurai sword!

"Where're you calling from, Len?" Frank spoke into the microphone.

"The Pine Glen area near Shoreham. Know where that is?"

"Sure, west of town. It's not much built up."

"Right. Just a few scattered houses and farms. The station wagon's parked outside a house on Locust Road."

"You think it's the same one you saw here?" Frank inquired, trying to avoid a false alarm.

Len Boggs sounded confident. "Sure looks like it. The license number starts with an X7."

"That's it!" Joe exclaimed excitedly as the combination clicked in his memory.

"Okay. Give us directions," Frank said.

Len Boggs complied, describing enough landmarks to make sure they found the spot.

Soon the Hardys sped off in their car with Takashi Satoya. The gray-haired Japanese recluse seemed to be enjoying the adventure thoroughly, coming more and more out of his shell as he traded remarks with Frank and Joe.

In less than fifteen minutes they sighted Len Boggs signaling to them from the road ahead.

"Any signs of life or new developments?" Frank said out the window as he braked to a gentle halt.

"Nope. The station wagon's the only car parked outside, and no one else has shown up," Len reported.

"Great! That sounds as though we ought to be able to handle the situation," Joe opined.

"Let's not take anything for granted," Frank cautioned. "Ikeda may have pals inside."

Satoya nodded. "It is always wise not to rush into danger."

After a hasty conference, they parked off the road and approached the house on foot. Well screened from view by trees, it was a modest white bungalow, bordered by tall shrubbery.

Len Boggs had agreed to ring the bell, since his face

presumably would not be recognized by Haruki Ikeda. The others waited out of sight nearby, huddled behind shrubbery.

Presently the door opened. Ikeda looked out with a suspicious frown. "Yes?"

The next moment he gaped in surprise as the others burst into view. Satoya called out what sounded like a command in Japanese and dashed toward the front door with the Hardy boys. Len Boggs stepped aside.

Ikeda tried to slam the door in their faces, but Satoya flung himself forward to push it open with his shoulder. The Hardys were close behind.

Suddenly Ikeda seemed to stop resisting their push. The door flew open under their combined weight, and all three went plunging inside. Their momentum carried them well into the front room, and they wound up sprawling headlong on the floor.

As Frank and Joe scrambled to their feet, they heard Len Boggs chuckle gleefully as he yanked the door shut behind them. The room seemed to fill with menacing figures, and the Hardys realized they had been lured into a trap!

Takashi Satoya rose calmly to his feet beside them. From his impassive expression, the gray-haired industrialist seemed utterly unperturbed by what had happened. But Frank and Joe felt no such confidence as they eyed the enemies who confronted them.

Besides Ikeda, there were five men, ranged in strategic fighting positions. Two were Americans—

Krunkel and another man, no doubt his partner in crime, Darbold. The other three were tough-looking Orientals with tattooed arms—obviously *Yakuza*, or Japanese gangsters. Among them the Hardys recognized the crook who had tried to shadow them in New York.

Satoya spoke coldly in Japanese, but his words drew a jeering response.

"Let's not waste time!" Krunkel growled in English. "Just grab 'em and tie 'em up—then we can figure out what to do with them!"

One of the *Yakuza* reached inside his suitcoat, as if to draw a weapon from a shoulder holster and cover the three prisoners.

But Satoya moved like lightning. He swept up a small table that stood within reach and hurled it through the air! It caught the threatening Japanese gangster on the side of the head and knocked him off his feet!

With angry oaths, the other crooks swarmed into action. But the Hardys and their gray-haired companion did not wait helplessly to be seized. They met the attack with flying fists and swirling aikido counter-moves.

In a minute the room was a bedlam of noise and violent activity. Ikeda, the gangsters and the two American burglars were far more dangerous opponents than the awkward, roughneck Gung-Ho gang had been. Also, the Orientals were expert enough in the martial arts to offset Satoya's fighting skill.

172

Whether the outnumbered trio could survive the battle looked doubtful. Frank and Joe realized the odds were heavily against them.

But suddenly the front door flew open and three black-clad figures burst in! A man in a business suit was with them.

"It's Sam Radley—and the *ninja!*" Joe cried.

The newcomers waded in, swinging punches and karate chops in all directions. In a few minutes the fight was over, and all six crooks, including Haruki Ikeda, were being lined up against the wall and frisked.

"What a break!" Frank panted. "You sure showed up at the right time, Sam! How'd you find this place?"

"Easy." Sam grinned. "Krunkel returned to the motel, then he and his partner came out again about an hour after you and Joe left. I think they may have gotten a phone order to come to this house. Anyhow, I trailed them here and then went off to find your dad."

"Where is he?" Joe asked.

"Three guesses," said a familiar voice.

One of the black-clad figures peeled off his hood, and the boys saw that the speaker was none other than their father, Fenton Hardy!

"Good night!" Frank exclaimed in astonishment. "When did you become a *ninja*, Dad?"

Mr. Hardy chuckled and gestured toward his black-clad associates. "I'm not sharp enough to call myself a *ninja* yet, son. But these two gentlemen have been giving me some mighty useful training. They're old army buddies of Mr. Satoya's. He uses them as his private security team."

"So that's where they came from!" said Joe.

Mr. Satoya explained that because at first he had suspected either Kawanishi or Oyama of being the traitor in his company, he had also been suspicious of the American detective whom they had hired to protect him.

The two *ninja* had been sent to the USA before his own arrival in order to prepare for his "disappearance." Later they had been instructed to keep an eye on the Hardys, and after Humber's newspaper interview, the wealthy collector had also been placed under observation, in case he might have been involved in the gallery theft.

It was through Satoya's secret request to the Japanese ambassador in Washington that the FBI had pulled Fenton Hardy off the case. Eventually, however, the famed private eye had convinced the two *ninja* agents of his trustworthiness—and since then he had been cooperating with them.

"But there's still a good deal we don't know about this case," Mr. Hardy concluded. "I'm hoping you boys can clear things up."

"I think we can explain part of the puzzle," Frank volunteered. "Ikeda hired the three gangsters to come over to this country beforehand, just like Mr. Satoya sent his two *ninja*. My guess is that the gangsters then hired Krunkel and Darbold to steal the sword from the Palmer-Glade Galleries."

"Right," said Joe. "But they also had a duplicate made, so they could switch it for the real sword and make Mr. Satoya look like a phony when he couldn't open the secret compartment, because the hilt of the fake sword *had no secret compartment!*"

The ransom ploy, so the Hardy boys reasoned, had been a clever way of getting the fake sword accepted by the police without anyone questioning its authenticity.

Had Warlord bought the fake sword, the police would no doubt have been tipped off by a secret phone call that they would find the stolen weapon in his possession.

When this move failed to work, the Hardy boys and Dobert Humber had been lured to Lookout Rock for a second ransom ploy. This time the crooks had taken no chances on anything going wrong, or themselves being trapped by the police. The siren trick had been used to make it look as though the thief had fled in panic, with the fake sword being left at Lookout Rock, where the Hardys would be sure to discover it.

"Smart thinking, boys," Mr. Hardy congratulated his two sons.

"A brilliant explanation, indeed!" Mr. Satoya agreed. "And now I think it is time to hear what my dishonest, worthless aide has to say for himself."

Haruki Ikeda seemed to shrivel under his employer's scorn as Satoya berated him bitterly in Japanese.

He confessed that for some time he had been engaged in crooked double-dealing, selling company secrets to its business competitors—especially Gorobei

175

Motors. The latter had used every means possible, including attempted murder, to keep the Satoya Corporation from merging its motorcycle division with the Road King Company.

In a last-ditch effort to prevent this from happening, Gorobei Motors had been pressing Ikeda to do something drastic. This had led to his clever scheme to have Takashi Satoya branded an impostor and removed from control of his own company.

The scheme had occurred to Ikeda partly because Toshiro Muramoto was worried that the company might already be in the hands of some crook who was merely impersonating the real Satoya. In fact, Muramoto had already been paying Ikeda for inside information on the company. He had done this in a sincere attempt to uncover any plot to take over the Satoya Corporation, without knowing that Ikeda was crookedly conniving with business competitors against his own firm.

But Ikeda admitted that the main motive for his scheme had been to make as much money as possible. He had planned to buy a lot of company stock after leaking the news story that Satoya was an impostor. This announcement would drive down the value of the company stock, so that he would be able to buy it cheaply.

He would then deliver the real sword to Satoya for a hundred thousand dollars in "ransom money." Once Satoya was able to clear himself and prove that he was the rightful head of the firm, the value of the stock would rise again. Ikeda would then be able to sell at a huge profit.

"How do these two birds fit into the picture?" Sam Radley asked the boys with a jerk of his thumb toward Krunkel and Darbold. "I mean, why were they hanging around this area after they'd pulled the museum heist and delivered the loot to Ikeda or his hired gangsters?"

"He probably promised them a share of the ransom money, besides whatever he paid them to steal the sword in the first place," Frank replied.

"Of course he'd have kicked in part of the ransom," Krunkel growled. "You think we're stupid enough to let him keep it all for himself?"

"Being criminals at all is stupid enough," Frank retorted coolly.

As Krunkel and his accomplice began talking, the Hardys learned that it was Sam Radley who had scared them into hiding the sword down the well. Once Krunkel started worrying that Sam might have identified him, the two thieves became alarmed that the sword might be found in their possession while they were waiting for Ikeda to take it to his employer under the pretense of having paid out the hundred thousand dollars in ransom money.

And as Joe had guessed, it was the news story about the recovery of the sword that had prompted Krunkel to check the well, because he and his partner had been

177

told nothing about Ikeda's scheme involving the fake sword.

"Well, that seems to clear up the whole mystery," said Fenton Hardy.

"Except for a certain document hidden in the hilt of Mr. Satoya's sword," Frank put in with a glance at the Japanese tycoon.

"Which I am quite impatient to check on," Satoya admitted.

After fleeing from the deserted farm in his rented station wagon, Ikeda had brought the sword into the house on Locust Road. It was lying in plain sight on the mantel.

The tycoon's expression was tense as he took down the sword. Frank and Joe watched in fascination as he gave the pommel cap a slight twist, then pressed two small metal decorations on the hilt, called *menuki*. Instantly the mother-of-pearl inlay on one side of the hilt swung open like a flap!

With a smile of relief, Satoya reached two fingers into the opening and plucked out a folded piece of paper. Without opening the paper, he borrowed a pipe lighter from Mr. Hardy and held a flame to the document. In seconds it caught fire and shriveled to ashes!

Frank watched him, suddenly feeling depressed. This was the end of their case. Would there ever be another one? He did not know that soon the boys would be called upon to work on *The Pentagon Spy*.

Suddenly a thought occurred to him, and he turned

178

to his father. "Dad, you didn't happen to see a motor-cyclist riding away from here, did you, or notice where he was going?"

"Matter of fact I did," said Fenton Hardy, "and the answer is nowhere—at least not for a while, till he spends some time under a pump, cleaning up."

"How come?" Frank queried.

"Because he ran into a farm truck and got trampled by a load of very annoyed pigs."

Once again the detective was mystified as he saw his sons burst out laughing!

You are invited to join

THE OFFICIAL HARDY BOYS ® FAN CLUB!

Be the first in your neighborhood to find out about Frank and Joe's newest adventures in the *Hardy Boys® Mystery Reporter,* and to receive your official membership card. Just send your name, age, address, and zip code to:

The Official Hardy Boys ® Fan Club
Wanderer Books
1230 Avenue of the Americas
New York, NY 10020

Don't Miss

THE HARDY BOYS ® MYSTERY STORIES
by Franklin W. Dixon

NIGHT OF THE WEREWOLF #59

THE PENTAGON SPY #61

THE APEMAN'S SECRET #62

NANCY DREW MYSTERY STORIES®
by Carolyn Keene

THE TRIPLE HOAX #57

THE FLYING SAUCER MYSTERY #58

Plus exciting survival stories in

THE HARDY BOYS ® HANDBOOK
SEVEN STORIES OF SURVIVAL
by Franklin W. Dixon
with Sheila Link

*Available in Wanderer Paperback and
Wanderer Reinforced Editions*